Concrete Killa 3

Kingpen

**Lock Down Publications and Ca$h
Presents**
Concrete Killa 3
A Novel by *Kingpen*

Lock Down Publications
P.O. Box 944
Stockbridge, Ga 30281
www.lockdownpublications.com

Copyright 2022 Kingpen
Concrete Killa 3

First Edition April 2022
Printed in the United States of America

This is a work of fiction. Names, characters, places, and incidents either are products of the author's imagination or are used fictitiously. Any similarity to actual events or locales or persons, living or dead, is entirely coincidental.

Lock Down Publications
Like our page on Facebook: Lock Down Publications @
www.facebook.com/lockdownpublications.ldp
Cover design and layout by: **Dynasty Cover Me**
Book interior design by: **Shawn Walker**
Edited by: **Nuel Uyi**

Stay Connected with Us!

Text **LOCKDOWN** to 22828 to stay up-to-date with new releases, sneak peaks, contests and more…

Thank you!

Submission Guideline.

Submit the first three chapters of your completed manuscript to ldpsubmissions@gmail.com, subject line: Your book's title. The manuscript must be in a .doc file and sent as an attachment. Document should be in Times New Roman, double spaced and in size 12 font. Also, provide your synopsis and full contact information. If sending multiple submissions, they must each be in a separate email.

Have a story but no way to send it electronically? You can still submit to LDP/Ca$h Presents. Send in the first three chapters, written or typed, of your completed manuscript to:

LDP: Submissions Dept
P.O. Box 944
Stockbridge, Ga 30281

DO NOT send original manuscript. Must be a duplicate.

Provide your synopsis and a cover letter containing your full contact information.

Thanks for considering LDP and Ca$h Presents.

Dedication

To my Guardian Angel

I used to flash $ 'cause I wasn't used to having it.
Now, I flash business cards—**Kingpen**

Acknowledgements

First and foremost, thank you God for this amazing gift. It's a blessing that I won't let go to waste.

To my family: I love and miss y'all dearly. I think about y'all every day. I pray for y'all, hoping y'all can be a strong unit together. We're all we got, and without each other we're not a family. I'll see y'all in 2023. Free Tonibone!

Jon and Yahira, y'all no aren't family by blood, but loyalty overrides so much to me. Every time I call y'all answer. Whenever I need y'all, y'all are there. Loyalty over everything!

A few names that I keep in mind; these names are important to me because in some way or at some point, y'all have impacted my life for the better: Sam and Lil C, Franko Zay, Ro, Baby G, Deun, Li'l Moe, Double D, Chi-Town, Nemo, JJ, Kenny Wayne, 7-5, Lil Coop, Eastwood, Vucci, Big Will, Savage, Porky, Tru, Quakey, Uncle Ben, B-Ron, Vucci, BCS, GP, JP, Bullet, Magic, BooBoo, Kuda Bang, Jr, Jeron, KD, J-Red, Chico, Head, Richie, Mo City. To all the brothers in the system, remember to stay humble. Stay focused and remember: undying love!

To my fans, sorry this is so late. I really put a lot of time and thought into this novel. So much of what you're reading, I can personally relate to. I've played the penitentiary game and I've hurt a lot of people in the process. I am very apologetic for the hurt and harm I've caused. But, this novel will be the last of this series. I hope and pray that y'all really enjoy it. Leave your honest review, good or bad.

Joshua Kirby#2003156
Torres Unit
125 Private Road 4303
Hondo, TX 78861

Prologue

Eastwood

"We come from poverty, man, we ain't have a thing—" I rapped along to my favorite song—'*Pop Out*'—playing on *97.9 F.M. The Beat* was jamming tonight. I had my headphones turned up to the max. I started mumbling on the parts that I didn't know, then the DJ switched to a different song. I didn't like the song that came on, so I turned my radio down.

"McFee crawling down the ace!" I could hear Hotboy's voice from a distance. I jumped up and grabbed my hand mirror. By the time I got the mirror out the bars, McFee was standing in front of my cell door. He looked at me and smiled. I looked up at my celly, who was sitting with his legs Indian-style, just staring at me. His fat, bitch ass knew Mc Fee was on the wing, and ain't try to tell me. I should have beat his bitch ass up when I had the chance.

I looked down at the brown paper sack that Hotboy had gave me to hold. I knew that I could flush whatever it was before McFee opened my cell door.

"Don't even think about it!" McFee said, as if he was reading my thoughts.

"The water is off, so—just hand it over, I know it's in there," he said.

I grabbed the pack off the floor and ran to the toilet. I pushed the toilet button, and nothing happened. I tried again, nothing

"Fuck!" I cursed. I was trapped, with no way of escaping.

Two more officers walked behind McFee to help him. "Just face the toilet, and make this easy on yourself," McFee instructed.

I dropped the pack on the floor and fell down to my knees. I cursed as I put my hands behind my head. I got caught slipping. But how? How did he know I had anything in here?

The door rolled as I awaited the cold steel cuffs that I had become accustomed to. McFee slapped his cuffs on me, then he bent down to grab the pack off the floor. "Take him to X-wing," he said. "I still have to thank his homie, Hotboy," McFee said, throwing me for a loop.

After being in seg' for a week, I was starting to get impatient. I replayed the whole night over in my head a hundred times. Hotboy has been my guy since day one. He was a real nigga. But when you say *was*, does that mean that he ain't no more? My mind was playing tricks on me. I had to blame it on the walls that had me closed in. Being in a cell was already bad as it was. But being in a cell alone—that was devastating. I didn't have any food, or my radio. Bitches wouldn't even give me anything to read. My neighbor snuck me a *Time* magazine. I read the bitch from cover to cover, twice.

"Eastwood!" a porter shouted my name two cells down from me. He pushed the broom in front of my cell door. "Eastwood!" he said.

I nodded. "Yea, what's up?" I asked.

He used the broom to sweep a kite under my cell door. "Hotboy," he said, as he walked off, pushing the broom. I snatched the kite up and unfolded the paper.

What's good, homie? I hope you back there staying sane. I want you to know I took care of that leftover piece of business. No witnesses! I know the way shit looks but I want you to know, everything ain't always as they appear. I'm doing everything I can to get you from the back. So, bear with me, one love. HB"

I ripped the kite into pieces and flushed it down the toilet. I had heard the alarm blaring last night. Crazy that the alarm came from Hotboy. I knew the lil' homie was solid. McFee liked to play dangerous games. If dangerous games was what he wanted to play, then let's play!

Kingpen

Chapter One

Lt. McFee

I parked my Mongoose Trail Bike and chained it to the bike rack. I stared at the entrance to the Beto Unit and sighed as I made my way to the front door. It's been almost a month and a half since the incident that occurred at C.O. Kiles' house. I was given a two-month vacation to help me recover from the tragic occurrence that took place that day.

Since the incident, I've been replaying that day over and over in my head, wondering if I actually did the right thing. I mean, I actually got the GI locked up, who's still currently awaiting trial in a federal jail. Not only did I rat him out, I also got an inmate killed. After everything happened with Kiles getting shot and killed, Kingsley passed away right before my eyes. The last time I saw him, the paramedics were rushing him out of Kiles' basement as they tried to resuscitate him.

"Hey, Lieu!" Ms. Warham greeted me as she walked behind me.

I nodded and held the door open for her. I was actually dreading this day. My first day at work. I knew every C.O. and the inmates had heard the story of what had happened that day. I walked through the door; all eyes were on me. I nodded and moved through the pat down section. As I bypassed the pat search, I walked through the door to get inside the main building. I took a deep breath. The inmates' hallway still smelled the same. It smelled like bippy and pine oil.

I walked in the Captain's office. Everyone in the room started clapping. The head warden, assistant warden, Major Cubea, Major Saks, followed by a bunch of sergeants. I looked around the room. I noticed a lot of officers were now wearing sergeant bars on their collars.

When I left on vacation, I was told that a full investigation was conducted on the unit. I was told a lot of ranking officers quit, for whatever reasons. That explains the new African sergeants.

"Lieutenant, good to have you back," Major Cubea said as he sat in the Captain's chair. Major Cubea was black. He was the only black major in the region. I knew Major Cubea really hates me. I really gave him a reason when I got GI Thompson fired and sent to jail. I knew it would be just a matter of time before Major Cubea tried to get rid of me.

As everyone looked at me, I held my hand over my stomach. I was quite ashamed. Which was one of the main reasons I rode my bike to work. In a sense, I was actually cheating because my house was four minutes away from the unit. But the way I peddled, it took me fifteen minutes to get here.

"Major Cubea, it's good to see you too," I said. For some reason, as they all looked at me, I felt like I was the outcast. Like no one wanted me here.

Major Cubea sat up in the chair. Everyone in the room stood around him like he was the warden. Even the subordinates stood behind him like he was the king of the castle. Maybe they looked up to him because he was the last black man standing with his type of rank. Beto had other black ranking officers. Captain Bortes was a large bull dyke woman with thick thighs, wide hips, and a flat ass. From the back, she looked like Suge Knight with dreads. But from the front she looked like Queen Latifah from the movie, *Set It Off.*

There was also Lieutenant Mark. He was tall, and heavy-set with misery legs. What I mean by misery legs was that it looked like the woman from the movie *Misery* got ahold of him, placed a center block between his legs, and hit them with a sledgehammer. His shit was that messed up.

The only other ranking C.O. that was black was Sergeant Greenwood who was bumping clits with Captain Bortes. The rest of the ranking officers who were black were African. Even though they shared the same skin color, they had different thoughts and different morals. Basically, the blacks and the Africans didn't get along. The only thing they had in common was beating the inmates up. But what C.O. did not?

"We didn't expect you to actually come back," Major Cubea said.

"Yes, I know, I'm back early," I said.

"No, not 'cause you're back early," Major Cubea said. "We," he said, then looked around the room and continued, "didn't expect you to come back at all, considering the traumatic incident, and the rumors that followed."

He really wanted to go there. My first day back, and I'm back early, and he's already taking shots at me. I guess there is such a thing as a good cop and a bad cop. I could tell which side he was on by the smirk that he wore on his face. I guess me and him had something in common. I didn't like him, and I knew he couldn't stand me either.

"I couldn't stay away. I couldn't sleep at night knowing I didn't finish what I started. I still have a long list of dirty C.O.'s I have to catch," I said as a few smirks turned into frowns. Now it was my turn to smile.

***

Memphis

As I stepped off the Blue Bird, I tilted my eyes and ducked my head to keep the sun from blurring my vision. I hated that I had downsized. I went from the big house to the little house. I had been paroled from Beaumont Federal, and now I had to start my state time at the unit everyone called Bloody Beto.

I lined up beside my pair as I watched this tall white sergeant say a speech that he probably recited in his sleep. I looked in his direction to give him the satisfaction of him thinking I was paying attention. As he finished, we all walked through the door to the back of the infirmary. I didn't care what hospital I ever went to; whether it was in prison or the free world, they all smelled like death.

The sergeant led us out the front of the infirmary into a long hallway that smelled of mush and K2. I looked around out of habit. No matter where I was, I made sure to know my surroundings. I could tell that I was going to have my way by how the inmates were acting. No one was in a straight line, and no one had their shirts

15

tucked in. I knew then and there that I was going to turn this bitch up. Even though I had heard multiple rumors about stabbing, and people getting killed, that shit don't faze me none. Beaumont Federal had stabbings every day, so that shit was normal to me. What I wanted to do was get to the bag. I had just found out that President Biden had just signed off another check for the stimulus plan. I knew damn near every inmate on the unit had signed up for it. The unit had close to 3,000 men. Subtract at least 1,000 inmates that didn't know their social or were illegal inmates. Still, 2,000 inmates with $1,800, with nothing to spend it on. I was about to give them something to spend it on.

The sergeant led us to a small room with four separate offices attached to it. Me and five other inmates sat and waited for classification to give us our housing, and job assignments. A sexy Caucasian lady with khaki pants and cowgirl boots walked out of the back room, and a bald Chinese guy behind her. He reminded me of one of those Triads from the movie, *Rush Hour*. He was dressed in crisp whites like me.

"Excuse me," I said as I stood up and placed my hands behind my back. Placing my hands behind my back was a force of habit. It was the federal way of holding a conversation without being threatening.

The lady looked at me as she chewed her bubble gum. I could tell it was about time she spat it out. "Yes," was all she said as she looked me up and down.

If she was looking for a flaw, she couldn't find it on me. My appearance was my everything. Big Boy Timex on my wrist. Gold Cartier frames over my eyes. Plus, I stayed starched down all the way down to my white New Balances.

"I'm just trying to see how this works, I just—" she stopped me mid-sentence and pointed to the seat I'd got up from.

"We'll be with you in a second. Sit down, and be patient," she said like she had a dick between her legs. It shook my heart. If this was the Feds, she would respect me as I respect her. *Yes, sir—no, sir*. I had to remember where I was.

16

"Curry!" A voice called my last name from the next room. I stood up and stepped over my red chain bag and walked in the small room. I sat in the only available chair opposite a small desk.

"How are you, son?" a Caucasian man asked.

I looked around the room. "You talkin' to me?" I asked, confused.

"Who else would I be talking to?" he asked.

"I misunderstood you. I thought you called me, *son*." I laughed. "My daddy black as hell, so you can't be my pops."

The man looked at me as he turned red in the face. "I'm Warden Wheatly, and you'll go by whatever I call you," he said, upset. I could already see what kind of unit this would turn out to be. A modern day plantation. '*Yes, sir, master, no sir, master*' type farm.

It took everything in me not to call him a cracka K-K-K who says the word nigger in his sleep. I wanted to, but I knew the outcome. Seg' plus a major case. I didn't have time for all of that. I had plans, and I couldn't do it in seg'.

"My apologies, sir." I bowed down to His Highness. He even smiled, thinking that he had won.

The sexy Caucasian woman opened a green file and began to read from it. "Joshua Curry. You're coming from Beaumont United States Prison. I see you have—oh wow!" she said as she showed the file to the warden. "I see you have a very long track record of established relationships, and riot cases."

I sighed. "If you'll look deeper, you'll see that for six months, I've been clear of all drama. I've been tryna give my life a new meaning. I just want to go home and be there for my family. At Beaumont, it was kill or be killed. In Beto I'll be able to relax and get a trade. Who knows, maybe even a degree."

"And what about the women?" the warden asked.

I pulled my glasses to the bridge of my nose. "Sir, the tree doesn't choose the bird, the bird chooses the trees. Wherever you plant me, I have no control over these bird brain C.O.'s."

The warden lightly chuckled. "Give him a job. Put him in the sign shop. That'll keep him busy!"

"What wing is that?" I asked curiously.
The warden smiled and said, "H-Wing."

Chapter Two

Eastwood

I sat on my bunk and scratched a line of paint on the brick wall, indicating that I'd been in segregation for yet another day, making it a month and twenty days. I had gained a full goatee. My head was as nappy as sheep's ass. The only plus was that I had gained a sense of peace and lost a little weight. The solitary time really helped my mind. I was smarter, more understanding, and deadlier. Doing solitary time let me see the mistakes I made before I came back here. The shit I used to waste my time on. The people that used to show love to me—they abandoned me. Since Hotboy died it's been only me. Come to think about it, being alone ain't that bad.

A pair of handcuffs banged on my cell door. I looked to see a face that I had killed in my head over a thousand times. I pushed up off the bed with my knuckles. I walked up to the chicken wire door and spat right in Lt. McFee's face. He wiped the spit and did not utter a word. Bitch ass cracka killed my homie.

"Get the fuck out front of my cell, pussy!" I said.

"I was coming to—"

"Get the fuck away from my door!" I yelled. I could hear the handcuffs clicking in his hand. He had to be a damn fool to think he was putting me in any kind of restraints.

"I just want you to know that no charges will be brought against you, and you're going back to the population. H-Wing, if that's where you want to go." He sounded like a changed man.

"How many times do I have to tell you, cracker! Get away from my fuckin' door!" The more I yelled, the more pissed I became.

McFee stood at the door. He stared at me like he wanted to say something. Instead of speaking his mind, he put his head down, and walked off. Cautiously, I walked to the chicken wire door. I was hesitant, thinking he would come back to mace me. As I stood in front of the door, a heavy-set Caucasian woman walked up to my cell.

"If you want to go to the population, pack your things. If not, I don't care. You can stay back here and rot. Your choice," she said.

"Where am I going?" I asked.

She looked at the move slip. "H-Wing."

***

Memphis

I walked on H-Wing with my property and mattress. All eyes were on me as I walked up the stairs to my cell. The cell door was already open as I walked up. My celly was in the cell moving his things around to make room for me. I waited until he stepped to the back of the small cell before I carried my things inside.

"What's good, homie? I'm Kingpen, that's P-E-N." He spelled it out for me. I tossed my mattress on the bottom bunk along with my chain bag.

"You can call me Memphis." I shook his hand then asked, "How is it here?" I laid my mattress flat on the bunk and set my property on top of it.

"It's well," Kingpen said. "It's all up to you. Beto is how you make it."

I took my prison-issued clothes off. I kept on my commissary shorts and T-shirt. I placed my right foot on the edge of the bunk and tied my shoelaces up tight. Kingpen looked at me. "What's up?" he asked.

"Getting ready," I said.

"For?"

"My check," I said.

Kingpen laughed. "They don't do checks on this unit. "They do but not our kind, not the blacks."

I looked at him, confused. "If y'all don't do heart checks, how will y'all know who's about that life and who ain't?"

He shrugged. "When something pops off, is when we find out," he said. "You bang?" he asked.

"I'm vice lord. U-V-K, Ghost Mob!" I recited with my chest out. I was proud of what I was. I represented my nation to the fullest.

Kingpen nodded. "That's what's up. It ain't too many vice lords on the unit. Maybe four at the most. There's a few Latin Kings, and one or two P-Stones."

I nodded. "I'ma check in with them. Let me go to the dayroom to see what the bidness is."

He nodded and dap'd me up. "Whenever you're ready to put up yo' things up, let me know, and I'll get out yo' way."

"Fasho," I said as I looked out of the cell before walking out. That was another habit I had. I was overly cautious from being in the Feds. Two reasons: one, I didn't know if someone was coming and I didn't want to bump into them. They could be holding their food, or a cup of hot coffee. The second reason: I didn't know who the enemy was. Niggas sit back and wait to catch another nigga slipping.

I walked out the cell, down the stairs, and waited in front of the dayroom by the door. A somewhat tall black female C.O. walked out the officers' closet and looked at me. Being new, I didn't know what to say. She put her hand on her hip and popped her gum. Her eyelashes blinked, her hand on her hip, as she popped her gum. Her eyelashes blinked like the wings of a bird. Her hair was freshly done, lace front with her baby hairs gelled to her forehead. Her name tag read: *Alex*.

"Mhm, lil' black. You tryna go in there?" she said. I laughed right in front of her face. She sounded like she was straight from the projects. She tilted her head to the side and popped her gum, her hand still on her hip.

"What's funny, black?" she asked. I was feeling this unit already. I would've shot at her, seeing the type of vibe she had, but I wanted to see what else the unit had to offer.

"I'm not laughing at you, Ms. A. Don't misunderstand me. I'm just enjoying yo' vibe."

"She looked at me up and down. "I like those glasses. What kind are they?"

"Cartier's," I said.

"Cartier glasses—I won't even peek at you, lil' black," she said as she pulled the dayroom door. "Don't go startin' no shit now, lil' black," she said as she opened the door.

"Trouble is something I stay far away from," I said as I walked in the dayroom."

"Uh huh, we'll see," she said, closing the door as she walked back to the closet.

I looked around the dayroom. It was smaller than Beaumont's dayroom. Beto didn't even have a paddle ball table in their dayroom. Only tables, phones, two TVs were here. They had to be no bigger than 40-inch TVs. I sat on the front bench beside a brown-skinned guy who resembled Kevin Gates. He was looking at some pictures; he looked up at me and said:

"What's good?'

"What's up?" I responded. I wasn't aggressive, but I wasn't friendly.

"I'm Lil D." He held his hand out.

I shook his hand. I noticed Beto was nice. Which was good. It meant that I now had a chance to make parole without killing someone. In Beaumont, the first thing they did was check your paperwork, then your name from the streets.

"Call me Memphis," I said. I watched the TV as Steven A. Smith talked shit on *First Take* about the Cowboys. I always like when he talks down on the Cowboys. It amazed me that they were America's team. Impossible, considering I was an American, too.

"Where are you comin' from?" Lil D asked.

"I'm comin' from Beaumont Federal. This shit already looks like a downgrade." I was proud that I had survived the worst prison in Texas. When I was told that I was going to Bloody Beto, which everyone called the worst prison in Texas, I laughed. They must've never heard of Beaumont Federal.

When I told Lil D where I'd come from, he looked at me with respect. "Oh, yeah, what's Beaumont like?" When I finished, he shook his head. "Well, it ain't like that here," he said.

"What's Beto like?" I asked.

"This bitch really like the projects. I'm talkin' 'bout rats, roaches, bitches, dope, and money. It's like the world, no bullshit. We do everything but drive cars, no cap."

I smiled. That was like music to my ears. "That's what's up. That's all I'm tryna do, get to the bag, and stay out the way, if possible," I said while still looking at the TV.

"It's possible. This Beto shit too easy. Watch, you'll see. I can tell you got some *playerism* about yo'self, so you'll fit right in."

He spoke the truth. I was a playa. But I wasn't tryin' to fit in at all. I wasn't tryna standout, just quietly run up the bag and fuck a few thots in the process.

"You bang?" he asked as another inmate stood under the TV, blocking his view.

"I'ma vice lord," I said.

"That's what's up. "Yo' people over there at the second to the back table." I could tell he was trying to look past the inmate that stood in his way. I was about to ask him what he banged until he said: "Say, cuz! You ain't made out of glass. Let everybody else watch TV." I knew right then and there the answer to my question. The inmate apologized, then stepped to the side so that Lil D could see. I stood up.

"Let me go holla at them," I said as I dap'd Lil D up.

Walking in the direction of my homies, I saw them look up at me. There were four of them sitting at the table. I tried to look at their tats to see if I could notice something; there were a bunch of stars, flames, and dog paws. I noticed a few P's and B.S.V on them as well. I walked up to the table and stood in front of them.

"What's poppin five?" the light-skinned guy who was playing chess asked as I walked up.

I looked at him like he was crazy. For a second, I thought Lil D was setting me up. I walked up to a table to a group of guys that's supposed to be my homies, and they straight up disrespect me, and what I stand for.

The light-skinned guy looked at me and said, "What's poppin five?"

I grilled him and said, "That five ain't never popping."

He looked at me and said, "You a blood?"

"I'm a vice lord, and where I'm from, saying *what's poppin five* is disrespectful," I explained.

He nodded. "Where are you from?" he asked as he moved a chess piece.

"Memphis, Tennessee," I said.

He nodded again. "That's my fault. You knew shit different out here. I ain't mean no disrespect." He extended his hand to me. I tried to shake it, but he did something different with his hand.

"What was that?" I asked.

"We look the five with y'all. As allies," he said.

This shit was getting weirder by the second. I just nodded. I knew different states banged differently. I was a long way from home, I had to remember that.

"So, how does this work with us?" I asked to be sure.

"Basically, we aid and assist y'all, and vice versa," he explained.

I nodded. They wouldn't have to aid and assist me, 'cause the only thing I planned and doing was get to the bag.

"What do they call you?" he asked.

"Memphis."

"I'm V-Doggie." He held his hand out again. I shook it; he did the handshake he did the first time. I was going to have to get used to it. "This is Mack, Divine, ReRe, but ReRe's none-active. The rest of the homies are at work, or school."

I shook their hands. The one who V-Dogg called Mack dap'd me up. I didn't know what his deal was, but if only he knew, I preferred to dap than to shake hands, and it had nothing to do with the Corona virus.

The front gate opened. A chubby, dark-skinned guy walked on the wing with his property. The homies stood up. V-Dogg walked up to the bars and said: "Eastwood! Damn, dog, it's good to see you."

Eastwood nodded and dropped his mattress as he leaned against the dayroom bars to catch his breath. "Who is speaking over here?" Eastwood asked.

V-Dogg looked at Divine and said, "Divine."
"Not anymore!" Eastwood said. "I'm the speaker now!"

Kingpen

Chapter Three

Anastasia

This shit was already getting on my nerves. I couldn't believe they literally thought this fake ass karate shit would work against some hardened criminals. They had to be crazy as hell to think I was going to try this shit on one of the inmates. I was tired of this workout crap. I was looking forward to my favorite part of the day: walking through the hallway.

Walking through the hall was the best part about being in the academy. The training sergeants kept reciting this ole *inmates-are-this, inmates-are-that* crap. To me inmates were humans like us, period. Twenty minutes later, after doing some more fake karate defense moves, I got my wish. We all lined up and got ready to go to the ODR, which was the officers' dining room. I wasn't hungry but I figured I might as well go cool off in some A/C. This gym was hot as hell. As we all lined up, I smiled. This time, the sergeant made me and my friend—Jay—get to the middle, close to the back, then he instructed another female C.O.—Hallward—to go to the very front. His reason was: the three of us made the inmates rush to the windows. In a sense, he wasn't lying. Me, Jay and Hallward were the youngest, and we all had an ass that turned heads. All three of us wore super tight pants. But I don't see why they were mad; hell, they issued us the pants. Hallward was Caucasian; she was about five foot four. She had a perfect shape for a white girl. What made her stand out as a white girl was her ass. She had an apple bottom. Jay—now that's my bitch, light-skinned ass. She had the juiciest ass out of all three of us. Her stomach was so flat that you'll think her ass was fake. It was real though. As for me, I was the youngest, probably the youngest, out of the whole group. I was only twenty years old. I know I was too young to be working in a maximum security prison. Being that I'm from Palestine, working in a prison was normal. It is one of the only decent paying jobs we had. It was either work here or peel the skin off of frozen chickens at Sanderson Farm. I got my nails done too much to be skinning some frozen chickens. But, my body, oh Lord! I hate to brag about myself, really I don't. I worked hard for my body. I worked out in the gym at least three times a week. I was a pole dance instructor on weekends, so I had to stay in shape. People always told me I had a flat stomach, with a teardrop booty. They often compared me to the singer Teyana Taylor. I would always tell them Teyana wished she looked as good as me. Even though I had a smaller ass than Jay and Hallward, I knew how to move mine better than both of them together. I guess it is in my generation to dance and should I say *twerk*! As we walked down the hallway, we caused a scene. In every dayroom window, inmates were kissing the glass and knocked on windows to grab our attention. Me and Jay laughed. It wasn't funny to the sergeant, but to us it was. I appreciated a man that appreciates my body.

As we made it to the E, F, G, H block, it was the same thing, the inmates looked but they aren't courageous as the A, B, C, D block. I put a little extra swag in my walk and pulled my pants higher, making my ass look bigger in my tight pants.

I laughed all the way to the O.D.R—me and Jay both. It was funny to us both; we were used to niggas hitting on us, but not like this. As we made it to the O.D.R., I was amazed at how this one room looked better than the whole unit. It actually looked like it wasn't attached to the unit. The floors were made of black and white tile. The floors were shiny as hell from all the wax. There were three large dispensers, one for lemonade, one for juice, and one for water. There was a 60-inch flat screen mounted on the wall with tan small tables surrounding the TV. Jay walked up to the buffet line and looked around at the different dishes. I stood behind her as she placed her hands on her hips. The food did look good. There was a platter of chicken lasagna, garlic bread, greens, baked potatoes, and something I couldn't recognize.

"Bitch, you gon' eat with me?" Jay asked me, and I shook my head.

"Naw! You know I have to keep my stomach on flat-flat." An inmate grabbed a tan plate and filled it up with chicken lasagna along with garlic bread sticks for Jay. I shook my head.

"Jay, you don't need that shit. Everything you eat goes straight to your ass."

Jay made her ass jump one cheek at a time. "You should get a double portion then." She laughed at her own joke.

"Don't do me, bitch. Big ass or not, you know I'm still that bitch."

Jay grabbed her plate as we found a table ducked off from the rest of the group of C.O.'s.

"So, what do you think?" she asked. "It don't look like a bad unit. These guys are thirsty, the male C.O.'s are thirsty. Other than that, it looks okay."

"What does it matter to you? You're going to be working at Telford, not Beto."

"Do you want to trade? Hell, I hear Telford is the jungle," she said.

"Nawl, I'm fine. I'll stay here." We both laughed. I looked around. This unit will be my new job in a couple of days. I was hella excited. I knew what my job description was: Provide a safe living and working environment for the inmates and C.O.'s. But I had my own agenda in mind.

Lt. McFee

Beto wasn't the same. At least not the C.O.'s. I could tell the majority of them hated me now. Everyone except the two new members of the unit's shake down team, which are called the *Hit Squad*. I was the head of the team. My second- in-command was Wangolo, a Nigerian from Niger. Then there was Grizints who was Caucasian like me. I had a plan, and I needed their help to make my plan a success. We were going to uncover every rock and look behind every hiding spot to clean up the Beto Unit. I was going to finish the job I started out to do.

As I sat at the two-twenty desk, which is basically a brick desk in the middle of the halfway where we see cases, I watched as C.O. Grain walked on the unit. She closed the door. I noticed she didn't have her work clothes on. She wore a pair of Levi jeans, a shirt with the word *Pink* on it, and some pink and white Nikes. Her hair was in a ponytail that hung down to her shoulders. She stared at the ground as she walked in the captain's office.

"Lieutenant, how are you?" she asked. She looked different, like down.

The last time I saw her was the day Seth kidnapped Kingsley; he was helping him escape, then he kidnapped Grain in the process, though she was already aware of Kingsley's escape plan. Grain ended up telling me exactly what happened. I kept the story between us. I told her I wouldn't tell the police that she was a part of the whole thing, as long as she promised to quit her job at the Beto Unit, and she did.

"How are you?" I asked her.

She sighed. "I've seen better days, but I'm coming along."

"I understand. Uh—Grain." She looked at me straight in my eyes. "I know we agreed to keep your involvement a secret as long as you quit your job." She nodded. "I've had some time to think about everything, and I know you have children to take care of. I wouldn't feel right taking food from a child's mouth. So, if you would like to stay, it'll be fine with me."

She looked around and said, "This place reminds me too much of him. If I stay, I'll always be distracted with thoughts of him."

"You really liked him, didn't you?"

She smiled. "*Like* is an understatement; I worship the ground he walked on. He's—he was an exceptional man. One that can never be replaced."

"I never got to send my condolences to you or his family for his passing. I hope I'm not too late."

"No and thank you. I know he didn't like you."

I laughed. "He hated me."

She laughed too. "Yea, he did." Her smile faded. "I should go, I, uh—I just came by to pick up my last check. Take care, lieu, and thank you."

"You're welcome." She shook my hand, and I watched her walk away.

Grain walked out the captain's office with a white envelope. She nodded at me in passing. I felt sorry for her and the unborn child. *Another baby would be growing up without his father. A baby who was created in prison. I shook my head in disgust. Never again!* I thought to myself.

Kingpen

Chapter Four

Hotboy

If you're gonna break my heart, just break it / And if you're gonna take your shot, then take it / Take it / If you made up your mind, then make it / Make this fast / If you ever loved me / Have mercy. I sang the country song as I ended the 1971 Chevy Impala that I was working on. I didn't know anything about fixing a wheel alignment, but I had to try something.

Grain—well, she hates when I call her that.

I still do it sometimes just to piss her off. She pulled up in her Toyota Camry and parked in front of my Impala. She stepped out of the car and walked up to me. She still looked beautiful, just like the first time I laid eyes on her.

"Hey, babe." She kissed my lips. I still had oil on my hands. I pulled her in and kissed her passionately. She pulled away and smiled. "Wow! You missed me that much. I only went to get my last check."

"You can go to the bathroom to take shit, and I'll miss you." I laughed.

She pushed me. "Stop being so nasty. Where's the twins?" she asked as I wiped the oil from my hands with a dirty rag.

"They're in their room asleep. Diedra gave me a hard time as usual. She didn't want to take a nap. She wanted to come and help me fix the car." I laughed.

"She adores you; you know that."

I nodded and pulled her into my arms, forcing her backside to me. I leaned my back on the side of the Impala. "I know. I adore them both. I just don't want her to grow up being a tomboy. That's what Jr. is for. We have a son. She needs to do girl things."

Stephanie nodded in my embrace. She stayed quiet. "Are you okay?" I asked.

She nodded again. "Yes, I'm great. I saw McFee when I went to get my check."

I laughed. "Oh yea, what did he say?"

"Nothing, really. That he sends his condolences for your death, and that if I wanted to stay I could."

I laughed harder. "Fat bitch. I knew he was all teddy bear on the inside. Crazy how he still thinks I'm dead." Stephanie broke away from me and faced me. "Gianni, I think we should just leave Texas, and never look back."

"Steph, you know I can't do that."

"Why not? 'Cause you still want to make McFee pay." She huffed. "Would you grow up and let that shit go! For Christ sakes, you have a son on the way, you're free now." She started crying. I pulled her into my arms as she cried on my chest.

"Steph bae, I'm here with you. I know we have a son on the way, but you know I can't let McFee live. He's the only one that can tie you to me. He has to go."

She lightly punched on my chest as she cried. I held her tight to me. "No! No! No! You don't have to kill him; you just want to."

"Steph, he has to go. Point blank period. He knows too much."

"Sometimes I don't know who you are."

I kissed the top of her head. "I'm that same nigga that you met in the pen months ago. The same nigga that stole your heart when you had it heavily guarded. But this is the side of me that I try to keep away from you."

I learned that I had this other side to me on Beto.

It was like I had another person inside of me. A Killa. A *Concrete Killa.*

"What if something happens to you?" she asked as he looked into my eyes. "I don't want to lose you. I almost lost you before, I don't—" She started crying again. "Please, don't make me feel that ever again."

I kissed her lips. "I won't leave you. I didn't the first time, did I?" She shook her head. "I know what I'm doing, I got this." We shared another passionate kiss. I grabbed her ass through her jeans as she moaned and lightly bit my lips.

"Now go in the house and make us some dinner. I'm starving." She smiled and wiped her tears.

"You got it, daddy."

As she walked in the house, I felt the gunshot wounds that were a permanent reminder in my life. I couldn't help but think back to how I got the wounds and how I beat the system.

"Gabby!" I said as I hadn't seen her in months. She was crying as she saw me walk down the basement stairs. I looked at Seth and asked, "What did you do to her?" She looked like she had gone through hell and back. Like he had been torturing her.

"The same thing I'm going to do to you," Seth said to me as he fired off a shot, hitting me in my right shoulder. The shit hurt like hell. Stephanie screamed like she had been shot.

"You piece of shit!" I grunted as I held my shoulder. It burned, like my shoulder was on fire; I could feel it going numb.

"Tell me something I don't know!" Seth said as he squatted down in front of me. "Tell me why you picked my fiancée, of all the women in the unit! You could've had any woman you wanted, but you picked mine!" Seth squeezed the trigger again; he hit me in my chest. The force of the bullet sent me back. The pain was instant.

A white woman walked down the stairs and stared at me as blood dripped from the corner of my mouth. I opened my mouth to speak. It hurt just to breathe.

"Bruh—I didn't mean to—" I managed to say as I wiped blood from my mouth. "I didn't mean to come between y'all."

Gabby cried as she watched the life slip from my body. I was in pain, and my body wanted to give up and die, but my will and pride wouldn't let me die. Not by the hands of Seth. He knew it too. I could tell by the way he stared at me.

"Kiles, please! Don't kill him, please!" Stephanie begged. A white woman walked behind Seth and whispered something in his ear. "Okay," Seth said to the woman. "Take everything to the car." She nodded and walked off. She bumped into a little boy. It was the same little boy I saw on Gabby's Facebook page. "Jacob!" the woman said happily. She noticed a gun in Jacob's hand. "What are you doing with that?" she asked him.

"Mommy," Jacob said with the gun in his hand.

"Yes," the woman smiled as he walked closer to Jacob. "I'm your mother." She touched his face with the palm of her hand. The gun went off. "No, you're not!" Jacob said as he dropped the gun.

The room was silent. Everyone stared at Jacob in shock. As soon as the woman's body fell, I was all over Seth. Seth had the upper hand on me, though; my injuries gave him advantage. But injury or not, I wasn't going out without a fight. Seth caught me with a few good punches. Stephanie came out of nowhere and jumped on Seth's back.

"Ahh, bitch!" Seth yelled as Stephanie bit into his cheek.

Seth slung her little body over his head, and blood dripped on his cheek. Seth aimed his gun at me and fired a single dot. He barely missed me. He fired off, and another couldn't hold me up. I fell down to one knee in pain. I raised my left hand, not out of plea, but out of instinct, like I could block the next shot.

"Seth—please!" Gabby begged.

Seth aimed his gun at my head. He looked at her and said, "Fuck you and him!" His finger went to the trigger, then a gun sounded, but I wasn't shot. I opened my eyes as Seth looked at his chest. Blood colored his shirt. He fell down to one knee as he looked at me. A single fear fell down his cheek. He looked exhausted. He gasped one last time then his body fell over.

"Gianni!" Stephanie shouted as she ran over to me with the gun still in her hand.

I was laid out on my back. I could barely breathe.

"Grain—tha—thank you!" I muttered.

She cried and said, "I tol' you, stop calling me that—You know my name," she said.

I smiled and said, "You kept your word—You got me out."

She laid my head on her lap as tears fell down her face.

"You hear that, babe?" Stephanie asked. I listened as the sound of police sirens got closer.

"I'm not going back to prison; I'd rather die!" I said.

"You can't, babe, you can't leave me. I'm pregnant!" She surprised me.

I looked up at her with tears of joy in my eyes. "Are you serious?"

She nodded and said, "It's a boy!"

I looked at Gabby then back to Stephanie. "We're naming him Gianni Kingsley, the third."

Stephanie looked at me, confused. "The third? I didn't know you're a junior."

"I'm not—But I had a son, and his name was Gianni junior."

The basement door swung open, and a gang of police officers ran down the steps with their guns drawn. I noticed a familiar face in the group. He walked up to me and said: "Gianni Kingsley."

I smiled a painful smile. "McFee, how did you find me?" I asked him.

"The van has a tracking device—We knew where you were all along," he said.

"Did you let my homie out of lock up?" McFee nodded.

"He's waiting for you to come back. He's on the wing, same as before."

"I'm not going back—I'm tired—I haven't rested in a long time. I think I deserve some rest." I gasped as I laid still on Stephanie's leg.

"Gianni! Wake up! You can't leave me!" She cried as her tears fell on my face.

That was why I didn't tell her the whole plan. I knew if I would've, she wouldn't have done exactly what she was doing or make it look real. The paramedics came in and placed my body on the gurney. There was one black male, and a Caucasian woman.

Stephanie held my hand tight as they raised the gurney to carry me up the stairs. "Ma'am, you have to let him go," the female EMT said to Stephanie. Stephanie cried as she let my hand go. I was carried up the stairs and wheeled right out the front door. I heard the back door to the ambulance open. The front of the gurney was pushed to the ambulance. The male jumped in the back of the ambulance.

"Can I ride with his body, please?" Stephanie begged. The male EMT nodded, and she stopped in the back of the ambulance.

The double doors closed, and the ambulance pulled off.

"Bitch, you know you heavy as hell, don't you?" the male EMT said.

Stephanie looked at him and said, "Who are you talking to?"

"I'm talking to Hotboy." Lakewood took his mask down and tossed it on the floor. "The coast is clear; you can get yo' ass up!"

Stephanie looked at me. I had a smile on my face. "Oh, you better not!" Stephanie said. "You faked your death!" I sat up on the gurney as I winced in pain.

"That was the whole plan, wasn't it?" I said.

She punched me hard in the arm. "Ouch, damn!" I shouted.

"She did right, you should've told that girl, you could've given her a heart attack," Mama Dee said from the driver's seat. Lakewood walked to the front and sat in the passenger seat. He kissed Ms. Deun on the cheek.

"I had my reason why I didn't tell her," I said.

Stephanie sat down beside me on the gurney as she kissed all over me.

"I thought you were gone. I thought you were dead." She cried.

I kissed her tears away. "I'm not going anywhere. I promise I have to be here for you and our son."

"Don't forget about the twins," she said.

I laughed. "Oh yea, them too."

"So, what now? Are you good? Are you free?"

"Not yet. This is just the beginning," I said.

She looked at me confused and asked. "The beginning to what?"

"The beginning to an end."

Chapter Five

Eastwood

Shit was about to change on Beto. By force or by choice. Losing my day one nigga—Hotboy—made me into a demon. That nigga was like family to me. Actually, he was more than family. My own family didn't send me money to survive in this hell hole. Hotboy gave me an avenue to feed myself. I was saving every dollar to get me a decent appeal lawyer. When Hotboy died, a part of me died.

There's a hundred rumors as to how he died. I heard them all. Some people say Hotboy was killed by the ex-C.O. Kiles. Some people say the police killed him as he tried to escape. The rumor I hated the most was the one about Hotboy being shot and killed by Lt. McFee. That was the rumor I used as the truth. It was the rumor that I used as fire to ignite my anger. The rumor I used to carry out my mission, even if it killed me.

I stood outside the day room bars beside my mattress and property. I looked at a few homies that surrounded the blood table. I recognized two of them, but the rest were new faces. Since my stay in lock up, the population had changed. A lot of homies had been shifted off. B-Crazy had got shipped to the wall unit. JJ had got G5'd for a phone case. Florida had got moved to another wing, and Los had got moved to another unit.

"Big boy!" the C.O. working the wing called after me. "Are you going in the cell or the day room?" she asked as she walked up to me. Her name tag read: *Alex*. She had to be new, because I had never seen her around.

"I'm going to the day room but I'ma leave my shit right here until I get back." She nodded and popped her gum.

"As big as you are, ain't nobody gon' touch it." She led the way to the day room as I watched her frame. She was tall, slim, and dark-skinned. She had smooth, pretty skin. But she had an ugly booty.

She opened the dayroom door. I stepped inside as she locked the door behind me. I nodded to Lil D who was a crip from my city. I walked up to the blood table and shook up with Divine.

"What's popping?" I greeted them. I locked B's with all of them except one person. Instead of locking B's with me, he tried to dap me up.

"He's new," Divine said. He's not from Texas, he's a vice lord." I felt everyone knew the way bloods shake with vice lords. He tried to do the handshake, but it looked funny, so I showed him. "It's like this—" We did it twice so he could get it down packed.

"What do they call you?" I asked him.

"Just call me Memphis," he said.

I looked at Memphis. He reminded me of Hotboy. Except Memphis wore gold Cartier glasses with a Dallas swag.

"I had a lil' homie that used to be here. He was from Memphis, too. A vice lord, too. You kinda favor him," I said.

"Oh yea, that's what's up. Did he put on for the city, or wha'?" Memphis asked.

"Did he?" I said as I smiled, thinking about my lil' nigga. "You got some big shoes to fill," I said.

Memphis nodded. "Don't worry. I'm hell fo'real. Whatever he did, I'm twice as worse."

I nodded. "Call me Eastwood." Memphis nodded. I looked around the table. "What's your name, homie?" I asked an old-school cat that resembled Martin Lawrence. He had thin wavy hair; he was going bald close to his hairline. I never understood that. Niggas be trying to save the little hair they have, no matter how embarrassing it looks.

"Mack," he answered.

"Where are you coming from?" I asked.

"I came from Coffield," Mack said.

"I heard Coffield was live."

"Yea, it's straight," Mack said. "I came over here 'cause my homie B-Crazy was over here. I found out I just missed him."

B-Crazy? You know him?" I asked. A lot of niggas claimed to know B-Crazy 'cause if you did, you gained a little clout because B-Crazy was a penitentiary legend.

"I've been gone twenty years in the system. Me and that white boy have popped off riots together and beat up C.O.'s together. I'm surprised he's never told you about me."

Now that he mentioned it, I did recall B-Crazy bringing his name up a few times when we traded war stories.

"Now that I think about it, he did say your name a few times."

Mack smiled and said, "That's my guy."

"So, what's up? Can somebody lace me up about this place?" Memphis asked.

"I just got out of lock up. A lot has changed since I've been gone. But when I was out, we had a little beef with the Crips behind some bullshit ass rumors."

"That shit squashed now," Divine said.

"I ain't gon' lie. I ain't talking 'bout no beef. I can handle all smoke that comes my way. What I'm asking is, can a nigga get paid over here?" Memphis asked.

"It's some money here. I know that for a fact," I said.

"What about the hoes?" Memphis asked.

"Depends on yo' game. Some will choose, some won't. The ones that won't choose will write you a case for attempting to establish a relationship. But looking at you, you look like you got a little *playerism* about yo'self."

"A lil'. Mane, Memphis stands for *making easy money while persuading hoes in style*. Breaking bitches is what I do. White— Black—or Mexican!" Memphis said, making me laugh.

"Damn, I swear you remind me of my nigga, Hotboy," I said as I thought back to how Hotboy used to break hoes like it was nothing. I shook the memory off.

"On a more serious note, shit about to change over here. The way the C.O.'s used to handle us, that's goin' to stop. See niggas be talking about that gangsta shit; in due time, you'll be able to prove it. That's why I'm takin' over as speaker for the wing. And if anyone has a problem, just say so," I said.

Everyone remained silent. "Divine, you fucked up?" I wanted to make sure.

Divine shook his head. "Nawl. In fact, I'm glad, 'cause I wanted to slide back and do my five percenter thang fully. So, now's the perfect time to say, I'm sliding back."

"Well, Michael Jackson then!" I said. "Once you moonwalk, ain't no coming back."

Divine nodded as he picked up his poetry book and drawing materials he used to make love cards with. He left the table without looking back.

"Now that the confusion is gone, we can get to the point at hand—" I was saying, until Mack interrupted me.

"Don't you want to wait until everyone gets back from the sign shop? We still got a lot of homies that's not here."

He made valid point. "You're right. I'll wait, 'cause I don't like repeating myself." I looked around. "I'ma go put my shit up in my cell. I'll holla at y'all later."

***

I walked to my new cell. I was housed on two row, in cell twenty-one. I wasn't used to being on two now. For one, my fat ass hated walking up the stairs all day; secondly, I had heat restriction, I didn't want to pass out in the hot ass cell. But, luckily, they blessed me with a single cell. So, I wouldn't be with another inmate.

I slid the door open and laid my mattress on the bottom bunk. I laid my property on the top bunk and took the hot ass state-issued shirt off. My body was covered in sweat. I pulled the door, making it look like it was closed.

I sat on the bunk and looked out the cell bar. I was back on H-Wing, back where I started. Except this time, I felt alone. All of my guys were gone. It was just me now. It didn't feel right, at all. Thinking about my guy—Hotboy—always got me in my feelings.

I sat at the edge of my bunk and let my head fall into my hands. *I'ma avenge yo' death, Hotboy. By any means!* I thought to myself.

Chapter Six

Memphis

They were calling chow at the same time sign shop workers were filing from work. It was like damn near the whole wing worked in the sign shop.

"You heading to chow?" Lil D asked me.

I nodded and said, "Yea, I ain't gon' eat. I'm just gon' check out the scene. See what I come across."

"I'ma ride with you if that's cool."

"Yea' fasho. Say, mane, I'ma playa-type nigga. I can see you a playa type nigga, too! I normally don't hit the streets with anyone, but you probably can lace me up and be one hunnit about it."

Lil D nodded. "I gotcha. But I have to tell you, what hoes might be good for me might not be good for you. Feel me?"

"Overstood," I said as we walked out the gate and made a left to go to the South chow hall.

"Memphis!" a big heavy-set, light-skinned guy who resembled Uncle Phil from the TV show, *Fresh Prince*, called my name like he knew me.

Inmates walked around me as Lil D waited for me on the wall. "You don't remember me, do you?" the big guy asked. I shook my head as I stared at him. "Big Tank!" He said his name. "We were on some tank in Dallas County. Remember, I used to wear the orange escape jumper. I used to sell cool-offs to you."

When he said *cool-offs*, it all came back to me. "Oh yea, Big Tank. You were the one that used to fuck with Ms. Willis." I remembered him like it was yesterday. Big Tank was the first person that I had ever seen win a C.O. in the system. He was the one that inspired me to chase C.O.'s. I remember Big Tank eating fried chicken and pork chops in the county. It wasn't much, but it was free world food. And he got it, A-O-A-B—all off a bitch.

I slapped fives with Big Tank as we shared a laugh. "Damn, old school, this where you were the whole time?" I asked.

"Yeah, I've been here for a few years. I fought in trial until they hit me over the head and gave me double digits. Hell, they shipped me here as soon as they found me guilty. By the way, what wing they got you on?"

"H-Wing."

"Me too. You'll like it, once you get the hang of the routine. What job did you get?" he asked.

"They got me in the sign shop."

"You might not like working there."

"Why do you say that?" I asked.

"Ain't no woman out there. Well, there's two, but they ain't yo' speed. But stay in there a week or so, and I'll pull som' strings to get up a better job."

I shook his hand. "Preciate it. Let me go though, check out the scene." He nodded and waited in the pill line.

"You know Big Tank?" Lil D asked as we walked in the south chow hall.

"Yea, we were in Dallas County together a few years ago, he a good nigga. Back in the day he used to be the tank boss." I laughed, remembering how Big Tank got his name.

"Yea, he a cool nigga. He keeps me laughing."

I looked around the spacious chow hall. There had to be over thirty tables in all. The foul odor in the air made me sneeze. It smelled as if a sewage pipe had burst in the middle of the chow hall. And as I looked around, it did. Inmates were stepping over thirty feet of water as they tried not to get dirt on their white soles.

"Damn, this where y'all eat at?" I asked disgustedly.

"I'on be eating this shit. I just stepped out with you," Lil D said as we waited in line.

As we waited in line, I looked out the glass that was lined up and down the wall. There was a clean long hallway that led to another building. "What's down that way?" I asked.

Lil D followed my eyes. "Oh, the O.D.R.—that's where the C.O.'s eat at. Their food tastes way better than ours."

As I looked through the glass, a group of C.O.'s was walking down the hall. They came through in small groups. Majority of the women were ugly as hell. Some were decent looking.

"Damn, that's sad." I shook my head.

"Yea, that's East Texas for you. Straight savages. If you catch a bad bitch from East Texas, it's most likely been ran through," he explained.

Another group came through. A Caucasian woman came through. Her pants were so tight I could see the camel toe clear as day. Two other Caucasian women were right behind each other. One of them had a big head with dirty blonde hair. The other one had brownish red hair. A chubby brown-skinned woman walked behind them. She walked as if she was walking on the side of her foot. As she passed the window, me and Lil D watched her ass.

"Got damn!" Lil D said.

I twisted my mouth and shook my head. "Now, I'm a man, but that's too much ass for me. I'on see how she wipe her ass. I know that booty filthy." I laughed.

"You ain't lying," Lil D agreed. "I know she got crumbs in her shit."

Another group came by. I watched this one chick as she conversed back and forth with a bright-skinned chick. She was sexy as hell. She had her hair in a ponytail. Her ponytail actually had a little hang time too. His skin was clear, no bumps or pimples. Her lips were juicy, coated in lip gloss. We locked eyes briefly; she smiled and walked by the window. I turned and looked at her walk away.

"Now, that's a damn!" I said.

Lil D nodded. "Look at the juicy booty beside her." He admired her friend with the bigger booty.

I shook my head. The lil' bitch had my dick praying for her pussy. She was that fine, I turned and walked out the line. "Where are you going?" Lil D asked.

"I saw all I needed to see. I'm going back to the wing." I walked out the chow hall door in a hurry to try to catch up with the sexy black chick. I was moving so fast I didn't walk in the line; I walked down the middle of the hall.

I spotted the chick, along with her homegirl. They were standing in the middle of the hall, facing H-Wing's gate. I smoothly walked up to them. I didn't smirk, smile, or speak. I just looked. Neither of them said anything; they both just stared.

The lighter one broke the silence. "Come here. Let me search you." She didn't have a name tag on. But her friend did.

I looked at the sexy one, whose name tag read: *Davenport.*

I faced the picket as I kept looking to my side at Ms. Davenport. I looked at her from her head to her juicy lips, all the way down to her—what the fuck! I thought she had a pair of Skechers. That was a no-no.

As the pat search ended, I stood in front of the wing until the keyboss led me on the wing. I looked back one last time, and eyed Ms. Davenport. I had to get her. By any means.

I walked to the day room. There were over eighty inmates in the dayroom now. They were all smiling and talking amongst each other. I walked towards the sports TV and placed my back against the windows. Lil D came and stood beside me.

It was early January, but it still seemed like summer was already here. I pulled my Cartiers off my face and held them out to Lil D. "Hold these for me real quick." I pulled my state-issued shirt over my head, leaving only my cool shirt on. Lil D handed my glasses back to me.

Lil D touched me on my shoulder, to get my attention. I looked in the direction of his eyes. The academy class was walking by to go home for the day. A lot of inmates scrambled to get to the window to get their last look for the day.

Everyone was pointing out who they wanted, or who they thought would be good on the dick, or who they thought would drop off. Me, I was looking for one chick—Ms. Davenport. I spotted her as she walked behind her light-skinned friend. While everyone was pointing to her friend's big ass, I was staring at her.

As they walked out of eye sight, I looked at Lil D and said: "I'ma get the lil' chocolate one. Watch!"

***

After everyone racked up that wanted to rack up, Eastwood called a ten-ninety. When he first told me they were having one, I looked at him, confused. I didn't know what the fuck he was talking about. He later told me that it meant meeting amongst the homies. It wasn't mandatory for me to attend, but I told him I would show up just to show my face.

They started off with a roll-call. I looked around the table; there were close to ten of them. After they did roll-call, the only names I could remember were Yellowstone, GP, V-Dogg, Mack, Waco, Savage, and Prince. The rest of them, I couldn't remember.

I introduced myself last. "I'ma vice lord, Ghost Mob. Three-star chief and enforcer. Everyone calls me Memphis."

We went around in a circle with me shaking their hands. Once we all finished, Eastwood started talking. "What's popping, homies? Some of y'all know me. All that's beside the point. I called this meeting, to tell y'all shits about the chance. From now on, I'm talking over as a speaker—all rules are in effect. There will be no fucking with punks, no stealing, no debts, and no drawing heat with the laws. If anybody does, it's an automatic violation. That includes me too. We ain't taking no bullshit from the guys, that includes the laws. If we see a homie get into it with a C.O., no matter who it is, we aid and assist. We gon' start at treasury, so when a homie comes in and he doesn't have anything, food or hygiene, we can bless him. Enforcer—" He paused as he looked around. "V-Dogg, you gon' be the enforcer. If anyone breaks the rules, they go in the bowl, and we ain't showing favoritism. I'on care if he is a bounty hunter, or a piru, or a vice lord; hell, Latin King, either. He fuck up, he gets popped."

V-Dogg nodded. "Shit's about to change around here."

Eastwood continued, "When I turn up, we're going to eat. All of us are gon' eat. When I bless y'all, if you fuck your shit off, don't expect a handout, you won't get one."

V-Dogg pointed towards the window. There was a tall, Caucasian with glasses looking at us through the window.

"Londers looking at us, so let's wrap it up," Eastwood said. "Does anyone feel like they want to slide back?" he asked. No one said anything. "Does anyone have a problem with the laws of the land?"

No one said anything. "Overstood. I got love for all of y'all. No matter what set you bang. I know how niggas be on that piru only shit or bounty hunter shit. I ain't like that. I'll die behind my niggas 'cause I know niggas that died for me," Eastwood said. He stayed silent for a second and said: "If nobody has anything to say then we are good."

Everyone shook up again as some of the homies departed. All that were left were me, Eastwood and V-Dogg. Eastwood looked at me. "What are you good at?" he asked.

"What you mean?"

"Do you grill tacos, make speakers, fix radios, what?" he asked.

I laughed. "What am I? Mexican?" I laughed again. "I know how to grill tacos, but it's never for sale. I fuck with ho's, that's my hustle. I break hos and put them on the team."

Eastwood nodded. "I might have an avenue. There's this lil' bright-skinned bitch that works up here. Her name is Sanderfield, she wears glasses. Last time I talked to her, she was cutting for a nigga," he said.

V-Dogg laughed. "That bitch got walked off."

Eastwood looked at him in shock. "Nawl, for real? When? How?"

"She didn't get caught bringing no pack in or fucking. She got caught stealing," V-Dogg laughed again.

"Stealing what?" Eastwood asked.

"Tissue."

Eastwood laughed. "Bruh, stop playing." He laughed again.

"I'm fo'real," V-Dogg said. "Okay, you know when COVID hit, the stores were all out of tissue. The world was going crazy for tissue. You know the unit supply room had close to ten thousand rolls of tissue for inmates. Well, one night, Sanderfield stole the key and loaded it up on boxes of tissue. The bitch went home and started selling tissue on eBay. The bitch ended up stealing three thousand rolls before they finally caught her. They started calling her the *cottonelle bandit*." V-Dogg made us all laugh. "She works at Walmart now, but they won't let her anywhere next to the tissue aisle."

I took my glasses off as I wiped the tears away from my eyes. That had to be the funniest shit I'd heard in a long time.

"Man, that hoe foul for that," I said as I continued to laugh.

"Damn, blood, I wanted to fuck that lil' yellow hoe, bad," Eastwood said.

"Yea, that's over with now. Unless you go on and catch her at Walmart," V-Dogg said.

As they talked about the chicks that were wired here or the ones that had got walked off, my mind drifted to Ms. Davenport. I couldn't help but wonder what kind of chick she was or what kind of C.O. she would turn out to be.

I'ma get her lil' sexy ass, I thought to myself, *by any means*!

Kingpen

Chapter Seven

The Following Morning

Memphis

My celly's alarm went off, waking me up in the process. I jumped up and looked at my own clock on the stand. The time read 4:00 a.m. My celly—Kingpen—stepped off the top bunk, placing his foot on the stool. He climbed down and turned his alarm off.

"Why you got yo' alarm set so early?" I asked.

"They call sign shop at 4:30. I get up thirty minutes early to get myself together.

I shook my head. "Are you serious?" I asked.

"Yeah, you should get dressed too. Your name was on the turn out list." Kingpen excused himself as he turned his back to me to take a piss.

I sat up in my bunk and shook my head. Four o'clock in the motherfucking morning. It wasn't like we were getting paid to go to work. This was modern day slavery at its finest. To make matters worse, I had aggravated time so I didn't get work time like non-aggravated people did. When they worked, as the days counted up, they were able to come home early. People like me with aggravated cases were slaved hard for nothing.

Kingpen washed his hands, brushed his teeth, and then washed his face. He put on his clothes, along with his black boots. He grabbed his face towel, a bar of soap, and his shower shoes.

"By the way, you can't take anything but your face towel, shower slides, and soap. Oh, and your cup and spoon."

"No food?" I asked.

"Not anymore, they used to, but they changed it up on us. So, we can only bring this, and a shot of coffee in your cup without water. You have to wait till we get out of there to put water in it!" he explained. Kingpen stepped to the side to let me get closer to the sink. I drained my snake to get my morning wood to go down. I washed my hands, then I brushed my teeth. As I finished, I heard doors opening and closing fast.

"Dropping out sign shop, and I'm not waiting!" the wing boss shouted.

The cell door rolled; my celly stepped out and headed down the stairs. I grabbed my shower materials and cup. I almost forgot my ID. I grabbed it, stuck it in my pocket and walked out the cell. I closed the cell door, locking it. I walked a couple of cells down to see if Lil D was awake to go to work. Him and his celly were both snoring.

Lucky bastard, I thought to myself.

I walked to the day room. The day room was packed like there was a Cowboys game on TV. Majority of them were smiling, shaking hands like they were happy to go to work. I walked over to the sports TV and sat down on the second bench.

ESPN was on as they replayed the top ten plays of the night before. I looked to the side of me. A dark-skinned chunky guy sat beside me. He stood up and tied a black shoe string around his pants like a belt. I shook my head and thought, *Country ass nigga.*

The guy sat back down, then he looked at me "You new?" he asked.

"Yea, I just got here yesterday."

"Kenny," he extended his hand.

"Memphis."

"Oh, you from the same state as them trash ass Titans," Kenny said then laughed.

"Watch yo' mouth. What, you a Cowgirl fan?" I teased. Kenny's faced turned sour. "I just met cha but don't get on my bad side talking about my boys." He laughed.

Me and Kenny talked about sports for the next thirty minutes until they started calling us out for work.

"One row, sign shop, let's go!" the wing boss shouted with the day room door open.

"That's my row," Kenny said as he stood up, grabbing his shower materials. "I'll see you there." He dapped me up and walked out of the day room.

I stood up and waited until they called two rows. I yawned and stretched my arms out. I was still tired as hell. It seemed like as soon as I went to sleep, my celly's alarm went off. I know now that I would have to go to bed earlier.

"Two rows, let's go!" the wing boss said.

I waited until a good amount filed out so that I would see where they were going. As we walked off the wing, everyone was lined up in front of the south shower door.

A tall Caucasian old man was calling off everyone's names in alphabetical order. "You'll be before me, right behind him." My celly pointed to a bright-skinned guy with glasses.

I nodded and fell in line. The C.O. called off my name. I stood in front of him. "ID," he requested.

I pulled my ID out and showed it to him. "Okay, go ahead." He nudged his head towards the shower.

I walked in the shower. There were six men dressed in plain clothes. Two black, and four Caucasians. "You new, boy?" a tall black man with three different shades of blue asked. He patted me on the shoulders, indicating he wanted to pat search me.

"Yea, I'm new. Just got here yesterday." He looked inside each one of my shower slides, then he handed them back to me.

"Call me Doc," he said. I wanted to ask him why he had so many different blues on. The nigga had on sky blue, royal blue, baby blue, and dark blue. To make matters worse, his nipples were poking a hole in his shirt.

"Where you from, Doc?" I asked.

"Right here in East Texas!" he said.

Figures, I thought to myself.

"What 'bout you? You from Dallas?" He looked at my shag.

"I used to rock a shag back in my days," he said.

Yea, probably with seven different purples too, I thought to myself.

I walked off in the direction of Kenny. "Lace me up, Kenny. What's it like out here?"

"It's cool. Some people like it, some don't. I've been out here for eight years. I do it to get off the wing. Make my time fly by."

I nodded. When I was in the Feds, I worked in intake for ten hours a day. It made my time fly by. "Who are the niggas in the free world clothes?"

"The bosses. They all have their own department. Basically, they're our babysitters."

I laughed. "Which one do you work for?"

Kenny pointed to the oldest boss out there. He was a Caucasian man who resembled John Wayne. "Is he cool?" I asked. I wanted to get the inside scoop, because if they were to place me with bullshit whip cracking boss, I was gonna quit, right on the spot.

"He has his days. I really like the department more than the boss. I work around some cool guys."

"So, who's the best boss?"

Kenny pointed to a shorter Caucasian boss. "Price, he's the coolest of them all. He's laid back."

I nodded. I had already formed the plan in my head. If they did not place me in Price's department, I was off.

Two Caucasian women walked in the shower; both held clip boards. One was older than the other. "Who are they?" I wanted to know everything. For what I had planned, I had to know the ins and outs of everything.

"That's mama Moe, and Ms. Wills," he pointed. I laughed because he had that pointing shit bad. "Ms. Wills is the head count manager. The big boss. And mama Moe is the second-in-command, the assistant count manager."

I nodded. "Come on, they locked the gate and opened the door leading to the outside."

We walked outside. The air had a trash stench to it. But the breeze felt amazing, and the night sky topped it off. The sky was dark, with only one star in it. I stared because it was the first star I've seen in a long time. "Y'all do this every morning?" I asked Kenny who was paired up beside me.

"Monday through Friday. Same time."

The long line of inmates moved as we traveled around the unit until we reached the sign shop which was surrounded by its own barbed wire fence. Ms. Wills unlocked the gate as we filed inside, and up the stairs into the first warehouse.

The light was bright, blinding my vision as soon as we walked inside. The A/C was bumping and jumping. I was told to stand beside the microwave, me and two other new boots. I filled out a bunch of safety paperwork and signed my name. I handed the paperwork to another inmate.

"Aye, can you get me to work for Price?" I asked.

The Caucasian inmate nodded. "Yea. He needs workers in the crating department. Can you crate?"

I nodded. I didn't know what he meant by crate, but I still said yeah. "I'll see what I can do," he said then walked off.

The Caucasian guy had some pull because he got me put in with the crates. I was introduced to my co-workers. George, who had his entire face tat'd up. He was bright-skinned like the sun, so you could see those tats clear as day. T-Rex, who was a bald-headed black cat with blank man type glasses. T-Rex was cock-diesel strong, like he ate vitamins and steroids. Then there was Lil Deun who was from Houston. He was the youngest out of us, being twenty years old.

They laced me up on what needed to be done. We joked and laughed like we were all old friends. Before I knew it, it was count time. I followed behind Dean as we walked outside. The sun had rose, and it was hot. Inside the warehouse I couldn't tell because of the A/C, but as soon as I stepped outside, I got smacked dead in the face by the heat.

I stood beside Deun as we leaned on the rail. I looked around the compound with the sun up; I was able to see everything. I mapped out my plan as I looked around. I looked towards the trees in the distance. I tried to calculate the distance between the sign shop and the tall watch towers.

I smiled at Deun. "What are you smiling for?" he asked.

"This is gon' be too easy. Like taking candy from a baby."

Chapter Eight

Hotboy

I sat up in bed as I looked over at Stephanie. She was sleeping peacefully in a ball as she drooled on her pillow. I laughed as I got out of bed. I walked down the hall to check in on the twins. I cracked their door open; they were both sound asleep. I closed the door back and walked back into my bedroom.

I crawled on the bed and kissed Steph on the forehead. She squirmed in her sleep and faced me. Her eyes fluttered. She looked at the clock on her nightstand. "You're up early," she said.

"I know. I got to take care of something." I kissed her in the mouth, morning breath and all.

"Ugh, stop!" She pushed me. "I haven't brushed my teeth yet," she said, sitting up in bed.

"What does that mean? For better or worse, right?'

She smiled. "You talk like you 'bout to propose or something.

I removed my pillow from the bed. Under it laid three small black boxes. Steph looked at me with an O shaped mouth. She grabbed one of the boxes. Lifting the lid, she looked at the small single diamond ring.

"I figured I couldn't just marry you, so I bought the twins a ring, too. An eternal package deal."

Steph grabbed the other two boxes and lifted the lids. Her ring was bigger than that of the twins. The ma'fucka had eighty-six diamonds on it. Cost me an arm and a leg.

I took it from the stash that I had saved up hustling when I was at the Beto Unit.

Steph looked up at me with teary eyes. I gradually slid down to my knees. Her words got caught up in her throat like she was eating a peanut butter cracker sandwich with no water.

"G-Gianni!" A smile jumped on her face.

I held my finger up, stopping whatever she planned on saying.

"Stephanie, when I met you, you showed me nothing but love and support. You showed me that you're worth more than just a rider. You can take control and drive too. You did shit I know only a true gutta bitch could do." When I said *bitch*, she gave me a funny look. I laughed and continued. "You got me out the pen', by any means necessary, and now you're carrying my son, our son. There's no other *woman* I'd rather spend the rest of my life with." I laughed. "That's *women*, because of the other two divas."

She smiled and choked on her tears. She wiped them away.

"Yes!" she said.

I laughed. "You haven't let me ask you first."

"Yes! Yes! Yes! A thousand times!" She jumped up and tackled me to the bed. "I love you so much."

I kissed her morning breath away. "I love you more."

***

"What's good, bitch?" Lakewood gave me a hug as I walked up to his car. "Why you smiling so damn hard? I got some' on my face?"

I laughed. "Nawl, I just popped the question and she said yes."

Lakewood embraced me again. "I'm happy for your family. That's love. So, when you gon' send the twins to boarding school?" he joked.

I laughed. "Leave my little angels alone."

"You know them lil' girls are the second coming of the bad seed."

"They just don't like you. They adore me," I defended their bad asses. The twins—Kayla and Diedra—were a handful when they first met me; they treated me like I was an adopted brother that they never wanted. I won them over, constantly showering them with gifts, and by letting them stay out late when Steph told them it was time for bed. Steph didn't like it in the beginning; she felt that I was turning the twins against her. I had to show Steph that she wasn't the only parent anymore, and even though she gave birth to them, I would be there to help her raise them; so, I had a say-so in everything too.

"The feeling is mutual. I don't like their badass either. When Mama Dee has our little one, we gon' fight our kids." Lakewood made me laugh. I sat in the passenger seat of his new 2021 Corvette.

Ever since Lakewood went home from doing his bid, he's been up one. He's been the plug for every main drug in East Texas. He upgraded and moved Mama Dee into a nice country style home out in Longview. She was six weeks pregnant, and she was super excited. As well as Lakewood.

Lakewood cranked up his 'vette as the being silently purred to life. "Why you got me driving you to an interview, when you know yo' boy can set some' up for ya! You ain't got to work for no white man trash." Everyone thought I was dead; I've been living my life as Arnod Matthews a.k.a Lakewood. I put in application after application trying to find a job. Looking for a job in Lakewood's name limited me to McDonalds and Wendy's. Luckily, I saw a new hiring sign for TDCJ trash company.

"You're playing with fire anyway, trying to work for TDCJ," Lakewood said.

"It ain't like I'ma be working on Beto. All I'ma be doing is picking up trash dumpsters and emptying them into the trash truck. It ain't like I'ma be a guard or som'! Snitchin' ass better not tell her either, or I'ma kick your ass."

I told Steph that I had an interview, but she thinks it's in the next town over, doing warehouse work in Longview. She would probably have a bad heart attack if she was to find out I was trying to work for TDCJ.

I can already hear her words in my head. *"You don't like freedom, do you? You would rather see me walking by your cell asking, top or bottom?"* I laughed to myself.

"It isn't my business to tell her. But if she finds out, don't tell her I know."

We pulled up to a gas station that was attached to the Walmart Supercenter in Palestine. Lakewood parked and stepped out of the car. "Pump, I'ma pump," he said.

I placed my New York Yankees snapback on my head and got out of the car. Out of all the gas stations in Palestine, he picked the busiest one. The one majority of the Palestine population comes to.

I curved my hat at the rim to hide my face a little more. I took the gas cap off the 'vette and held it in my hand. When pumping gas, I stopped placing the gas cap on the hood of the car because I would always drive off, leaving the gas cap on the hood of the car. I can't remember how many times I did that shit.

I leaned my back against the car as I waited for Lakewood to come out of the store. The hot sun was making my head sweat under my hat. *Come on, nigga*, I thought to myself as I looked to the entrance of the store for Lakewood.

Lakewood walked out the store with a big smile on his face. He walked up to the 'vette and said, "Mane, you ain't gon' believe who works in there."

I really didn't give a damn. I knew he wouldn't give up until I pumped the gas. "Who?"

"The white girl with the fat ass. Sergeant Childs. And bruh, she looks even better in her khakis. She didn't remember me though."

"That's 'cause when you were there, all you ever did was jack off on 'em. They never heard yo' voice or know your face." I laughed as a silver dodge ram parked a few pumps away from us.

A sloppy built Caucasian with a TDC uniform got out of the truck with his back to us as he turned around. I walked around to the passenger side of the 'vette in a panic. I opened the door and yelled at Lakewood.

"Nigga, let's go!"

Lakewood looked at the fat white man. "That's McFee!" he said as he was getting in the car.

Lt. McFee heard his name and looked in our direction. Lakewood showed the parking lot what the Corvette could do as he sped out the lot, doing a hundred.

"Damn, that was close!" I huffed as I pulled my hat off.

Lakewood laughed.

"What's funny, nigga?"

"Bruh, if he would've seen you, he probably would've shitted himself. Seeing you would be like seeing a ghost. Remember, he saw you die."

I thought about what Lakewood said, and I got an idea.

Kingpen

Chapter Nine

Memphis

My fucking feet were hurting from them hard ass steel toe boots they made us wear. Instead of them protecting my feet, they did the opposite; my corns were busted.

"This is the part I hate," Lil Deun said as we lined up in the application department to get strip searched.

Getting strip searched had become like a daily routine in my life of imprisonment. I had gotten so used to it, I don't need clothes. I could walk around the compound completely naked and hold a full conversation.

I was just that in tune with my sexuality.

My name was called. I walked up to my new boss, Price. I handed him my clothes, one item at a time. He searched each item and tossed them to the floor. "How'd you like your first day?" Price asked.

I turned my back to him with my nuts lifted in my hands. He could see I didn't have any contraband hidden under them. "My first and last day. It was cool, but I'm more of a night time person. Y'all get up too early for me." I grabbed my clothes and shoes and walked off naked.

After we all got dressed, we walked back to the main building. We stopped at the back door as the C.O. called for a sergeant to escort us back inside. I noticed a few inmates in front of me had already started getting naked. I assumed they were getting naked for the shower, but I was wrong.

The sign shop bosses lined up and started strip searching us again. "Aw! Naw, never again!" I said out loud. This got to be some gay shit. The whole day all Price talked about was his wife and how he could never get enough of making love to her. He also had me rolling when he started rapping this throwback rapper named Twisted Black.

I grabbed my clothes and walked in the shower. I ran to the water and jumped under it. The water felt so good as it rained over my body. I hadn't worked that hard in all of my years in prison.

State prisons fucked up for not paying them niggas, I thought to myself. I wasn't no fool; I wasn't going back. Ever!

I finished my shower and got dressed. Majority of the sign shop workers went to lunch. I skipped chow. After a hard day of free labor, we were last to eat. What a shame! That meant we would be eating the slop of everything. The remnants. Nah, I'd rather eat plain Jane soup.

I walked to the gate to get on the wing. I felt clean. My shag was puffy, still wet from the water. My waves aren't crisp and laid but they were there. The keyboss opened the gate and let me on the wing.

I walked on the wing and tried to run up the stairs. I was stopped by the wing boss, Ms. Bee. Ms. Bee was in her mid-thirties. I knew because my celly—Kingpen—talked about her all night. He basically laced me up on all the cool laws, the laws that were good, and the laws that were not. He informed me that Ms. Bee was a freak. She would fade the dick like a pro. I didn't care about that. I was a Memphis nigga. All mackin', no jackin. Ms. Bee was pretty for her age. I just didn't like the cheap weave she had in her hair. The color didn't sit right with me.

Ms. Bee stepped to the side. I damn near floated to the chick behind her that sat on the orange cooler. It was none other than Ms. Davenport. She looked at me and smiled. I got lost in her big glossy eyes.

"What's your name? You new?" Ms. Bee asked me. I nodded, unable to get a word out my mouth

Here I was, a playa, a pimp from the land of pimping. I had two bad bitches in front of me, and I was at a loss for words. *Shake it off, Memphis*, I told myself.

Ms. Davenport stood up. I looked at her up and down. She was sexy as hell. Her body was banging. Her pants were so damn tight I could see her panty line from the side. I looked all the way down to her shoes. She still worked her Skechers like they were the latest Jordans.

I snickered by accident. Ms. Davenport looked at her shoes and boldly said: "Fuck you, boy, laughing at my shoes. I'on care, they are Skechers but they are comfortable."

I laughed and shook my head. *Ghetto fabulous*! "Uhm excuse me, you didn't tell me your name," Ms. Bee said.

I saw then she didn't want to be left out of the party. She wasn't one to let a younger sexier bitch outdo her, and I was enjoying the attention I was getting. Maybe it was the Cartiers, or just my Memphis swagg, but I sensed a little competition going on.

"I'on really know you to give you my government name, so just call me Memphis."

Ms. Bee laughed. "If I wanted yo' real name, I can get it."

"Whatever you want, I know you can always get it," I shot back. Even though I was feeling Ms. Davenport more, I wasn't gonna pass up the opportunity to win some bobcat. Some good ole wild adventurous pussy.

"At least you know." Ms. Bee smiled.

Another inmate called Ms. Bee to the dayroom bars. She excused herself and walked away. I watched Ms. Davenport as she sat back down on the cooler. She reached in her pocket and pulled out a pack of *Now and Later*, one of my favorite candies.

The whole time I kept looking at her. I couldn't help looking at her Skechers. "Uh—stop!" She noticed me looking.

"Babygirl, we can't have you walking around in Skechers. We gotta get you some Jays. What's ya cash app?" I asked.

"Naw, I'm good. I can take care of myself." She opened a piece of candy and tossed it in her mouth. I watched as her juicy lips smacked as she ate the candy. She stopped momentarily and took the yellow half of the candy from her mouth and sat it on top of the candy wrapper.

"That was the best part," I said.

"Uh, no it's not."

I grabbed the candy from the plastic and she stopped me.

"Gurl, you got AIDS or something?"

"No, but you nasty. That came from my mouth."

"So, if I'll kiss you, I'll eat out your mouth." I tossed the half chewed candy in my mouth as I closed my eyes like it was the best *Now and Later* I've ever had.

She held her hand over her mouth and crossed her legs. "Oh my god! You did not just do that, boy."

"I really did," I said as my celly—Kingpen—walked down the stairs towards me.

I dapped him up. "They shook our cell down. I think they got some of your stuff."

"I looked at Davenport. "Y'all shook my cell down?"

"What cell are you in?"

"Two-oh-nine," I answered.

"Yup and I got yo' freaky pictures too." She pulled them from beside her.

They were a bunch of freaky pictures my baby mama Jessica sent me when I was in the feds. Ms. Davenport looked at the pics. "She needs to work on her poses. That shit is so high school. Don't anybody sit on the bathroom sink anymore."

"Oh yeah, how do you take yo' pics then?"

She shocked me and stood up and bent over, facing me. Her ass was inches away from my dick. She held her hand over her head like she had a camera. "Like that." She smashed her lips and sat back down.

I couldn't help but laugh. "You wild, ma!"

She shook her head, laughing. "I'm me."

I took another piece of candy on my tongue and curled my tongue, hiding the candy behind my tongue. I wanted to show her what I could do with my tongue.

She crossed her legs. I knew I had that young pussy wet. If I had a thermometer I could've held it to her pussy and it would've read: *Devil Paradise*.

"So, let me get my pictures back?" I asked as I stepped a little closer to her.

"Nah," she said.

I laughed thinking she was playing. "Chill out, ma. Give 'em here."

She held them out and spread them like she was holding hundred dollar bills. I stepped between her legs; she looked up at me with lust-filled eyes.

"Memphis!" Ms. Bee shouted.

I eased from between her legs with a stare down. I wanted her to know she wasn't fucking with no little boy. I wasn't some scary inmate. I was free-world with my shit.

"Boy, you gon' get yo'self and her in trouble!" Ms. Bee said.

I nodded. I wasn't afraid of trouble. In fact, it was all I ever experienced in life. If she wanted trouble, then I was gon' give it to her.

Kingpen

Chapter Ten

Two Days Later

Eastwood

I walked to the dayroom feeling like shit. I wasn't under the weather. I was feeling like shit because I had plans to change Beto, but I couldn't do it without any work. All the C.O.'s I knew, they were all gone to different units, or scared to fuck around because of Lt. McFee. There were a few C.O.'s dropping work off, but they were already boo'd up with other inmates.

It was Saturday, so the unit was quiet. A lot of ranking officers were off on weekends, so the unit was basically deserted. Saturdays were my days to venture off up and down the unit to see if I could see from another inmate who was holding. Lucky for me, the African C.O. that was working the keys opened the gates for me. As I slipped off the wing, Memphis slid off behind me.

"Whoa, dog! Where are you going?" the African keyboss asked.

"Dadoo, he's with me. I got'em." Dadoo was a tall wide shoulder Nigerian who was ten minutes from being a full- fledged American nigga. Dadoo didn't want anything to do with any African women. All he craved was African American women. He loved two things: The word *dog*. And chicks that ate ass. Dadoo said he fell in love with America when his first African American woman ate his ass. Now, he never goes back home to Nigeria.

"Dog, let him know don't try me like that again," Dadoo said.

Lil Memphis looked like he wanted to snap back but he didn't. I nodded to Dadoo and walked off. "Homie, where you tryna go? You can't be walking off the wing like that without a pass. They'll write yo' ass up," I explained as we walked down the hall towards the north end of the unit.

Memphis adjusted his Cartier frames on his face and said, "I ain't scared of no pen and paper. Fuck they cases."

"You can't think like that, homie. Beto has its own culture. It's hard to catch a case here, but when you catch one, the rank will bam yo' ass.

Memphis shrugged. "Fuck a case. I'm here to make some money until crackers open the gate for me to go home."

I nodded. "I feel that."

"This bitch trash. Where the work at? Don't seem like nobody's hustling on this bitch. In the feds, niggas got pounds and pounds of dozier and tune floating around for sale. All I see here is that paper shit. And I'on smoke, but nigga still is giving me straight smoker prices."

"Niggas that still got work slow rolling it 'cause that fool McFee—He taking shit down."

"I heard about him. My celly Kingpen laced me up on that fool."

I looked at him. "Kingpen's yo' celly?" He nodded. "You got a good celly. That nigga play dumb, but he smart than a mu'fucka. Niggas be seeing them tats on his face and all over his body and think he a young hot head, not knowing he got a publishing contract with *Lockdown Publications and Ca$h Presents*!" I pointed out.

"Yea, he's a cool person. But I ain't gon' lie, that pecking on that typewriter gets on my nerves sometimes," he said, making me laugh. "But he knew a lot. He told me how McFee was taking niggas down left and right. If a nigga gets a chance to get in his office and snatch everything he ever took, a nigga would be on."

Lil Memphis' words gave me an idea. We walked a little distance until we got close to the barbershop. I stopped and looked towards Lt. McFee's office. "You sure you are not scared of a case?"

***

I looked around as Memphis used a flat head screwdriver and a spoon that I stole. I grabbed the screwdriver from the maintenance cart, and the spoon from O.D.R. Memphis claimed he knew how to break in with only those two tools. As long as he was taking, I doubted it.

"Damn, my nigga. You tryna get us caught or wha'?" I asked. Let me try." As soon as I said the words, the door clicked and Lil Memphis turned the knob.

He looked back at me with a grin on his face." I told you, Clepto!" He stood up and opened the door.

We walked inside the office and damn near fainted. There was another door. *Please God don't let it be locked, too,* I thought to myself. We walked up to the door. I turned the knob and sighed. It was unlocked. I felt around for the light switch. I turned the light on.

I didn't know where to start. I looked around. His office wasn't big. Certainly not big enough for his fat ass. He had two chairs. One for him and one for all the inmates he interrogated. His desk was cluttered with papers and half eaten snacks. His restroom was inches away from his desk. The door was open. There was a white toilet, a sink, and a mobile pressure washer.

I looked at Memphis. "What's this?" he asked as he looked at the bookshelf that had a bunch of different name tags. "Jones, Freeman, Valencia." I laughed. "Those were chicks that worked here. That fat bitch had a trophy case of all the C.O.'s he walked off, like it was a real accomplishment."

"Who's this?" he asked as he pointed to a torn out kite magazine page.

I looked closer. It was Sanderfield and another inmate that used to be on the unit. Sanderfield had put in the magazine that she missed and loved him. She looked good too, lil' bitch was rocking her pink haircut.

"That's the lil' bitch I was tryna get. That's the one that got walked off for stealing toilet tissue from the unit supply room," I said, laughing.

"If she got walked off for stealing tissue, how does the lieutenant know about the magazine?" he asked.

"One of them snitching ass inmates had to show him. Or they showed a C.O., and the C.O. showed McFee." I explained.

I started looking around for all the confiscated dope and phones McFee looked at over the years. I knew a lot of it had probably been turned in, but some shit he probably kept. I looked through drawer after drawer.

"Look!" Memphis held up two long shanks made from the cell lockers. "I'm keeping these hoes. Where I came from, they were mandatory." He stuck them in his sock and raised his sock up to his knees, concealing the shanks.

I opened all the drawers but one. I opened the last drawer and hit the jackpot. "I knew it!" I said as I pulled out the entire drawer and sat it on top of the desk.

Memphis stood beside me as we both started pulling out cell phone after cell phone from the drawer. I pulled out three cans of rolling tobacco along with at least a hundred sheets of paper tune. I sat it all beside the phones as I kept digging. I pulled out a file of pictures of inmates. They weren't pictures from the TDC database. They were pictures of inmates who took them with cell phones.

Dumbass! I thought to myself.

After we emptied the drawer, we had a total of fourteen different kinds of cell phones. iPhones, HTC, Verizon, Metro PCS, and some old-school flip phones. Six *Universal* phone chargers, six SIM cards. Four cans of tobacco. A zip of green K2, and over two hundred sheets of paper tune.

I looked at Memphis; he smiled at me and said: "What now?"

I grabbed a pen and paper. "What are you doing?" he asked as he looked over my shoulder.

"Leaving a *Thank You* note!"

Chapter Eleven

Lt. McFee

"Hey, lieu', you're here on the weekend. Bored at home?" Lieutenant Tru asked.

I sat in the chair across from her. "My wife's at the country club with her friends. You know how that goes."

Lieutenant Tru laughed. "I know. My ex-girlfriend used to go there and she'll stay gone all damn day. I went with her one time, and after the first time, I never went back.

I laughed as I thought about her ex-girlfriend—Ms. Kush. Ms. Kush had an amazing body for a white woman. Many nights I dreamt of catching Ms. Kush with some contrabands, so that I can see her get strip searched, or have the opportunity to pat search her.

I sighed. "This place isn't the same anymore," I said as I leaned back in the chair, placing my hands behind my head. "It's boring now."

"That's 'cause you took all the fun out of it," she said.

I looked at Lt. Tru. Her spiked Mohawk mullet made her look like a chubby porky pine; she reminded me of myself twenty years ago when I went to prom.

"How did I take the fun out of it? As I recalled, prison isn't supposed to be fun. It's supposed to be rehabilitated."

"Not fun for them. I mean fun for us. Back in the day it was fun chasing dirty C.O.'s and catching inmates with contraband. Now, it's a safe prison. Nothing really going on. You either walked all the dirty C.O.'s off, or you shipped all the conning inmates."

"I did what I was supposed to do," I defended myself.

"Then why do you look like you regret it?"

I sighed. "It's not that." I huffed and sat up in the chair. "It's just that I sacrificed a lot, my marriage, my ability to move around my own city. I can't go to Walmart without looking over my shoulder hoping I don't bump into an inmate that I took down. Then I sacrificed an inmate. All for what? To get the O.I.G. that was dirty too. Where's the good in that? Where's the honor in that?

"Sean, I heard about what happened with Hotboy." She held her hand up to excuse herself. "I'm sorry, Kingsley."

"It's okay, I know that you know a lot of inmates by their nicknames. When they thought I didn't, I never called them by their nicknames unless I wanted them to know that I was watching them."

"I play the cool boss role, to catch them off guard. I know what side of the fence I'm on," she assured me.

"But, Sean," she went on, "I heard about what happened with you and Kingsley. Everyone heard. But, don't you be walking around beating yourself up thinking that you got him killed. Kingsley was smart. Probably one of the smartest crook convicts Beto has ever housed. You thought you were using him to get O.I.G. Thompson. The whole time, Kingsley was using you to gain his freedom." She paused momentarily to drink her soda. "I wouldn't be surprised if Kingsley was in the free world on someone's beach with his black ass getting suntan lotion rubbed all over his skin."

Her comment made me laugh. "Oh, he's dead alright. I was there. I watched him take his last breath."

"And my mother gave birth to a daughter, yet I fuck women with a dick every night." She stood up and walked out into the hallway as she yelled at two inmates that were walking by.

I took the comment as it bounced around in my head. As I walked out of the office, I looked down the hall. I shook my head. There was no point in me chasing behind them.

There wasn't nothing major going on Beto anymore. I had made it safe for everyone to live smoke-free and in peace.

I walked to the north side of the unit to my office.

I pulled my keys from my pocket and stuck them in the first door to my office. The door opened without me having to turn the lock.

Damn, I thought to myself. Wangolo or Grizints fucking forgot to lock the door.

I walked in my office. The second door was wide open; the light was on. As soon as I stepped in the office, I knew the door being open didn't come from one of my own. I walked around my desk.

My bottom drawer was completely out of the desk as it sat on top of my desk on top of a cluster of paperwork.

I knew once I saw the drawer on the desk, I would find the inside of it empty. At least not completely. There was a note. It sat neatly at the bottom of the drawer.

I picked the note up. It read: *Let the games begin*!

***

Memphis

I was sweating like I had just finished fighting with Lucifer himself. I had a bundle of paper tune and phones tucked under my nuts. When the fat dike lieutenant yelled at me and Eastwood, I just knew we were dead. But when she didn't chase behind us, I sighed in relief.

As we walked on the wing, I followed behind Eastwood as he stood behind the stairs. I looked at him like he was crazy, wondering why we weren't somewhere getting this shit off of us.

"I don't want to run straight up the stairs," he said. "Niggas be watching, even when you think they aren't." He must've read my mind.

I looked around the dayroom. A few people did appear to be looking at us out the corner of their eyes while we were talking. "Come on, let's go," Eastwood said, taking the back half of the stairs. I followed him as he led us up the stairs to his cell.

"Look out for me," he instructed as he sat on his ass on the ground, placing his foot at the bottom of the cell door.

I looked over the rail in both directions as Eastwood rocked the door hard with his foot. The sound was loud, yet fast as he finally got the door open. He walked in, taking his shoes off at the door; out of respect, I did the same. I know some niggas were what you would call penitentiary. They didn't wear shoes, or shower slides in their cell. They kept them at the door, careful not to track outside dirt in their cell.

Eastwood grabbed his wool blanket and hung it up from the edge of the top bunk, to the nail on the wall. I ducked behind the curtain with him. Eastwood had already pulled out the contraband that he had tucked. I turned my back and did the same. He grabbed his floor towel and placed it on his desk. I laid the items I had on top of the towel.

"Damn!" was all Eastwood could say as he looked at the phones. "Pick you a phone, one just for you." I looked at him because there was only one iPhone. I didn't want to grab it and have him feel some type of way. He had to be a mind reader as he said: "I'on care which one you get, just pick one."

I grabbed the iPhone. Not out of greed but because I knew if they were to ever catch it, it was privacy approved. They would damn near have to get a warrant to get inside it. Eastwood picked a wide touch screen HTC phone. "Pick another one," he said.

I picked a widescreen flip phone. We went back and forth until we had six phones each, with one left.

"We'll use this one for the pound. Get it turned on and let the dogs rotate it. Feel me?" he said. I nodded. That was smart thinking.

Next, we divided the tobacco and chargers. We got two cans and three chargers each. Eastwood sat down on the stool and started counting the sheets of tune as I split up the leafy K2, using my ID, eyeballing it. After he finished counting the sheets, it came out to hundred and eighty-nine sheets.

"Give me ninety, you get ninety and split the rest up between the family," I said.

He shook his head. "Nawl, we can't let them know our play by play actions. This ain't the NFL network. I'ma use the last of this shit to pay the hold man. Unless you gon' hold your own?" he asked.

I had forgotten about where I would hide it. "Nawl, yea, good idea."

Eastwood laughed. "I thought you were a hustla. Looks like you are freezing up on me."

"It ain't like that. I'm just used to pack in the mail; it's game. As soon as it touches my hand, it's gone."

"What's the difference?"

"I'on really know anybody here. I'on even know what the price is on this shit." I looked at one of the sheets of paper.

"I'ma lace you up. These sheets, they can run from an ID card and easy quick hunit dollars. Or the whole sheet, you can boom it for five through six hunnit. These Jag, right now since McFee got the hoes scared to jump, we can't corner the market. We can sell them hoes anywhere from fifteen hunnit, to two racks. Them cans—if I was you I wouldn't wholesale them. Me, I'm gon' bust them hoes down and sell 'em for seventy-five a cap. Easy."

I nodded as I did the calculations in my head. With just the sheets alone, selling them at five hunnit—that would be a quick forty-five grand. But I knew me; selling them at five apiece would take forever. I already had my mind made up to sell them at three hunnit apiece. Like Eastwood said, *corner the market*. That was still a quick twenty-seven racks. Free bands! I was gon' sell four of my phones for fifteen hunnit apiece. The only reason I was keeping two: Just in case I ever had to flush one. Always gotta have a backup plan.

I watched as Eastwood turned two of his phones on. They were both plugged into chargers. "I'm tryna see if any of these hoes are still activated."

I did the same. I plugged a charger up to the iPhone and smiled as the screen came to life. My smile was soon shattered as the screen showed that the phone was locked. I showed the phone to Eastwood. "Look!" He looked at the screen and laughed.

"I already knew it. That's why I let you pick first." He laughed.

I laughed with him. I played myself. "It's cool though. "We can look at YouTube later and find a way to crack the code. It's always a way," he said.

I nodded and plugged in another phone. "I got a signal on one of these hoes." He showed me the screen of his HTC phone. "We on. All we have to do is get the rest of these hoes on, and we can up the price for doing it."

He looked at me. "I'ma need yo' help though. I'on got nobody on the outside I can trust that I can send my money to. I just met you, but if you anything like my nigga Hotboy, you a real nigga. A loyal nigga."

"Like I told you, whatever Hotboy was, I'm two times worse."

"Who can you get to hold all yo' money?" he asked, then said: "We 'bout to touch a lot of money, and it'll be the type of money that'll make a bitch do two things: hold you down or run off with yo' paper."

"I'on have nobody that'll do it without question, other than—" I paused, thinking.

"Who?"

I laughed. "My baby mama, Jessica."

Chapter Twelve

Jessica

"Princess, come over here and sit down so I can finish your hair, please!" I swear, this lil' girl is such a damn diva. Badass. I don't know where she got it from, 'cause I did not come up as bad as her ass. She had to have gotten it from her daddy, Joshua.

"Mommy, it hurts. You pull too hard." She scrunched up her pretty little face. Her chinky Asian eyes were tight, making her look like she was really mad.

"Girl, if you don't bring yo' ass so I can finish—the only way it keeps hurting is 'cause you keep moving. Now come on!"

She pouted and sat on the pillow that was on the floor between my legs. She folded her arms and stuck her lips out. I couldn't help but laugh. Spoiled ass.

I grabbed my iPhone from beside me and handed it to her. Her face lit up as she scrolled to her favorite game, and clicked on the app.

I was tryna get her tail ready for gymnastics. With the COVID slowing down, she was finally able to go back. That was all she ever talked about, gymnastics and her damn daddy.

My phone started ringing. Before I could reach for it, she answered it like she was grown. "Hello, this is Princess." She had the biggest smile. "Daddy!" She turned and looked at me.

I wondered how he was calling when I didn't see her accept the call. "Yes, I've been good. But mommy, she's got—"

I snatched the phone from her. She was always tryna snitch on me, like I was the kid and she was the parent.

"Hello," I spoke into the phone.

"Baby mama, you miss me or what?" he asked in his smooth Memphis accent.

Ever since we were kids in high school, that shit always had me worked up. To this day, it still does. "How are you calling me, Josh?" I looked at the phone and saw that it was from a 210 area code.

"You know I have my ways. What's up though? How have you been?"

I shook my head. I knew he was somehow on a cell phone. He did the same shit when he was in the FEDS. "You don't wanna come home to your daughter, do you?"

He huffed. "Don't do that. You act like I'm using these mu'fukas, I am on Netflix or some'. When I use 'em I'm handling business."

"What business you got, Josh, huh?" He always had an excuse. His ass never going to learn. Princess looked at me directly in my mouth.

"Princess, take your ass in the room, all in my mouth and shit. That's why you're so manish now."

I put the phone back to my ear. Josh was laughing hard as hell.

"That shit ain't funny, Josh. I swear, she had to act like you when you were a kid, 'cause she damn sho'll don't act like me."

"Blame it on me, huh. I'll take that." The phone went silent, neither of us saying anything. "So, who's ya new boo? I know you got one."

"Boy, if you called my phone to ask who I'm talking to, you better check yo'self, fo'real, Josh."

He laughed.

"A nigga can ask, can't I? Chill out, talking to me like you crazy." He made me smile. No matter how mad he would make me, I would always get over it quick. He had that effect on me.

"So, how are you doing in there? You okay? Did you get my letters and pictures? Princess wrote you a letter, too." I do what I could for him. Being that when he was free, he took care of his business with Princess and me. I told him that I would be there to help him through his bid, mentally and emotionally. And I would bring his daughter occasionally. Over the eight years he's been away, sometimes I would leave him hanging, mostly for some bull crap he's done. Like one time, he had the nerve to have a female C.O. send me some money. I accepted the money, until the bitch had the nerve to say she was fucking him. I sent the money right back to her country ass and told her to tell him to never call my phone again. About a day or two later, he called my phone from a cell phone. I knew it was probably a phone he got from the skank ass guard bitch. He ended up smoothing things over with me, explaining that he was doing everything intimate to her and with every stroke, he always envisioned he was fucking me. I know that last part was some straight bull crap. But I also knew he was a man. A man in prison. So, I know if a bitch threw some pussy at him, he would definitely catch it.

"Yea, I got them. I wrote y'all back. I sent it out yesterday morning. Y'all should get it by Wednesday. I ain't gon' lie you looking damn good, girl. That ass getting fat."

He made me laugh. "Boy, shut up. Do you see your daughter at gymnastics?"

"Yea. I noticed. When did she start back going? I thought it was closed down for COVID?"

"It was closed. They just opened it up like a week ago. I'ma take her up there when I finish talking to you." I looked towards Princess' room; she had her head peeking out the door, eavesdropping. I shook my head.

"I need you to come and see me tomorrow." His voice was as country as it could get. I love that shit about him.

"I can't tomorrow. I have plans to go out with my homegirl, Claire."

"Jessica, look who you're talking to. If I'm asking you to pull up, it's a reason I'm asking you to."

I sighed. "Okay, Josh, we'll be there."

"Do me a favor too. Do you still got some of that money I sent you when I was in the FEDS?"

"Why wouldn't I have it?"

"Well, bring me ten hundred dollar bills. I need it."

"Josh, why are you always doing shit? No! You don't need no damn cash in there. You just always tryna show people you the man. Would you just sit yo' ass down and come home!" I swear this nigga stress me the hell out sometimes.

"I'm coming home, by any means, ma. But, why not get this paper while I'm sitting here. What's the worst they can do to me— put me in a single cell where there's A/C."

I shook my head. If only he could see how pissed I really was. I knew preaching to him would be like preaching to the choir. One thing about this stubborn ass: once his mind was made up, no one could change it.

"Look, Josh. I'ma coming tomorrow, but don't expect me to bring anything else. You know I don't like doing that shit, especially when Princess's with me."

"Another thing," he said.

I sighed. "What now, Josh?"

"I need yo' cashapp"

"Why?" I kinda already knew why. I just wanted to hear him get mad. That shit always turned me on how one minute he could be hot then the next, cold as ice.

"Jess! Stop askin' so many mu'fucking questions and just do what I say. You startin' to piss me off!"

I laughed. "Yes, baby daddy!"

***

Anastasia

"Tash, I swear, Beto is live. You need to come up there with me. I can get you on up there," I said to my best friend Tasha.

We sat in some warm, comfortable black leather chairs as my nail stylist—Tameka—did my nails. I attended the nail salon, *Happy Nails,* every week to get my nails done. Between me partying, twerking, and working, I started tearin' my shit up. They didn't call it *Happy Nails* for no reason. 'Cause once you left, it would look as if your nails were smiling.

"A-D, I'm not going to no prison. I'm fine where I'm at," Tasha said as she played on her iPhone watch. She called me A-D because of my first and last initial.

"Gur', Walmart does not pay that good."

"And Beto doesn't either!" she spat.

"But I swear I will be having fun. Like, tomorrow I'ma be training on the second shift. They say second shift live." I was all excited.

"Bitch, you sound like going to Disney World or something."

"Never know, my prince might be on Beto. Yours too, maybe."

"Gurl, you know I'm strictly pussy. I don't do dick."

Tasha wasn't into men. Don't get me wrong; she would date them every blue moon, but she was more attracted to women. Sometimes, I would feel weird when I would be at her house getting ready for the club. Her eyes would be roaming all over my body. I had to remind her clit bumping ass that I was strictly dickly, wasn't gon' be no scissoring over here.

"That's even better if you don't like men. That means you can do your job without any distractions. 'Cause—woo! Gurl" I fanned myself. "Lord knows I am distracted."

"Let me find out you already crushing on somebody up there."

I laughed. "A few. But oh my God! Let me tell you about this one dude. His name is Memphis. Gurl, it's something about that boy. I swear, I had a dream about him last night. And that was the second night in the row."

Tasha laughed. "You are something else. That boy ain't doing you like that."

"Tasha, you think you like pussy; if you see this nigga, I swear you'll cross back over like Taylor Swift did with pop music. He'll make your pussy wet just by taking off his shirt."

"I'on know 'bout that. But I'll come up there. I'ma put in an application and see if they'll hire me up there. But, A-D, I'ma tell you, if I don't like it, I'ma leave."

Chapter Thirteen

The Same Night

Hotboy

"You sure this is where he stays?" I asked Lakewood as we pulled up to a country style home in Palestine.

"Yea, fool. Don't you remember you sent me to his house months back? I had to climb through the nigga window. Just so you know, I ain't doing that shit no more. Especially not in these shoes." I looked down at his new Gucci loafers. Them hoes were clean, but he was starting to sound like a straight bum.

"My nigga, all you got to do is watch out." I didn't wait for him to answer. I walked around the side of McFee's house.

After Lakewood broke into McFee's house the first time, McFee's scary ass went and bought some motion sensor lights. Them hoes were bright as hell too. Just what I needed to accomplish my mission.

I walked towards the house, setting off the motion sensor. As I walked around his house, I stood outside his bedroom window. I waved my hand, making the motion sensor go off. The bright light shined right on my face. "Come on, fat pig. I know you're in there. Wake up and shit your pants," I said to myself.

I stayed still. The light went off. I waved my hand again. The light came back on. I stared at the bedroom window, hoping someone inside the house would look out. I got my wish. The blinds at the bedroom window opened, and it was none other than Lt. McFee.

***

Lt. McFee

"Get him! He's on the loose! Don't let him get away!" I was talking in my sleep as I dreamt about an inmate trying to get away with contrabands. "Dangelo! Take the back stairs!" I mumbled in my sleep as I tossed and turned. I was woken up by a bright light that flared in my eyes. I blinked a few times to adjust my eyes, then I tried to block the lights as I walked to the kitchen. It seems like ever since I paid to have these darn lights put in, the damn rabbits and rodents kept setting the sensors off. It was starting to irritate me.

I walked in the kitchen and opened the refrigerator. I looked around for a late night snack. I grabbed a piece of my wife's homemade apple pie and scoffed it down. I opened the jug of milk and chased the pie down. Closing the refrigerator, I looked down at my stomach. I looked disgusting. My belly sticks out further than it ever has. My hips started to poke out like a girl and the eerie time I turned a corner, my man boobs would be two seconds behind sloping all over the place. My wife said she loved it, but that was only because she was fat too. *Get yourself together soon*, I thought to myself as I walked back to the bedroom.

The motion sensor light went off as I sat on my side of the bed. My wife snored light as she stirred in her sleep. As I was about to lay down, the motion sensor light came back on. "Fuck!" I mumbled under my breath.

With them damn rabbits running around, I'll never be able to get any sleep. I stood up and pulled the string to the blinds. The light hit me in the face like a punch. As my eyes adjusted to the light, I thought I must've been dreaming. I mean I had to be.

"What—the—fuck!" I screamed as I stared at a ghost. It was Kingsley. He was there, dead, alive. My wife jumped out of bed. One of her titties laid damn near on her sideways. I looked at her then pointed out the window. "It's—It's—Look!"

By this time, I turned back to the window and the light was still on, but there was no one there. My wife walked beside me and looked out the window. "What, Sean? I don't see anything." My mouth hung open. I know I'd seen him, or did I? Was I hallucinating? I had to be. Kingsley was dead. I saw him die. I saw his eyes closed. I heard him take his last breath. I watched the EMT's take his body out on a stretcher. He was, I know that for a fact.

My wife shook her head and walked back to the bed. "Sean, you're going crazy. I think it's about time you took a vacation from the prison." She laid down and covered herself with her quilt.

I shook my head. I need more than a vacation. I needed to see a therapist or a psych doctor.

***

Eastwood

I scrolled through my old Facebook pages as I looked up random C.O.'s that had worked here or used to work here. I can recall how at the unit barbershop other inmates would give their opinion on who was the baddest bitch to walk the unit. I had my own special few. So, to determine who's the baddest, I looked their page up. I started with my crush, Sanderfield.

I clicked on her page. She looked good. More than good. She was hands down killing something. She had a few pics with some mediocre photographer. Maybe she was tryna be a model. She could definitely model for a tissue company. I laughed at my own joke.

Next, I went to my second crush, Margarita. She was another dime in my book. I used to have a big crush on her. She used to give the fat Mack some major play. Her lil' skinny Latina ass had me sprung, too. I clicked on her page.

"Damn!" I said out loud. I sat the phone down and peeped out my spy mirror to see if anyone was coming. I didn't have anyone watching out for me because me and Memphis made up our minds that we could keep it a secret until Monday. People had heard that Lt. McFee's office had been hit but no one knew who did it. So, to keep our names clear, we decided to not sell anything until the heat wave went down.

I ran back to the phone excitedly. I looked at Margarita. She had got tat'd up all down her arms. She looked like the boss bitch she indeed was. "Umuh!" I shook my head, upset at myself that I never got to sample that pussy.

"What the fuck!" I muttered as I noticed she had a ring on her finger. I scrolled through a few more of her pictures to see that she had gotten engaged to some nigga in the military.

I shook my head. Can't turn a hoe into a housewife. She was friends with Hotboy's ex, Ms. Newton. I clicked on her page on my best nosey shit. I knew doing the shit I was doing was how a lot of niggas got popped. But at the moment I didn't give two fucks.

I scrolled down Newton's page. She had a lot of new pictures. She was back walking. It was her, and her step son Jacob. She looked happy. As I scrolled further down her page, she had a post that read:

RIP, Gianni Kinglsey, gone too soon.

The post was liked by Lt. McFee. I liked the post too. Thinking about my nigga always brought me to a blind rage. The way his so called friend slandered his name once he died! Like he didn't keep it real with only the real niggas.

I clicked on Lt. McFee's Facebook page. His profile picture was of him and his wife. I scrolled down his page. All of his posts consisted of something to do with Beto. Just seeing the smiles on his pictures made my blood boil. On one picture he stood with a group of SRT green suits as he shook one of their hands. In another picture he is presented with the employee-of-the-year award.

I shook my head and logged off my Facebook. "Employee of the year!" I laughed to myself. I'm making sure that never happens again.

Chapter Fourteen

The Following Day

Memphis

I laid in my bunk as I waited for them to call me for a visit. I had called Jessica on the jag' like ten minutes ago. She told me that she was pulling into the parking lot now. I sent my jag off to the hold man as I took a quick bird bath. I used my Gucci body wash. And once I dried off, I lotioned my body with my homemade lotion. I used a regular bottle of cocoa butter lotion, but I ripped out the cologne from a magazine ad. It was the Tom Ford cologne ad. I scraped the paper off into dust and emptied the shavings into my lotion bottle. I shook the bottle up and voila! Cocoa butter Tom Ford for prisoners! I could've bottled that shit up and sold it, but I wasn't into cosmetics-and- smell goods. I was a pimp and a trapper.

My celly—Kingpen—sat at the desk as he always did, typing. I swear that nigga sometimes got on my nerves with that shit. If he wasn't reading a book, he was either writing one or typing one. I wasn't hating on him, 'cause his shit was on fire, but it was the *tck, tck, tck* from that damn old-school ass typewriter that annoyed the shit outta me.

"Kingpen, homie, take a break, please, for me!" I begged. He laughed and stood up, stretching in the process.

"I'm like ten chapters away from finishing up another novel. This hoe fire, too." He sat on the toilet and yawned. The nigga would be tired and still would type.

"Oh, word. What's the name of it?" I was curious. I mean I didn't like the ticking noise, but I supported his dream. The lil' nigga had a helluva vision.

On many occasions when I wasn't on the jag talking to baby mama, or Princess, me and him would ride. It would be mostly him talking, but he'll have my undivided attention. He would tell me about his dream of starting his own magazine. His dreams of writing movie scripts and one day owning his own publishing company. He

would always talk about moving to Atlanta with his publisher—
Ca$h—and make it rain at the strip club: *King of Diamonds*. That
part of the story would always grab my attention.

"The name of this one is called, *Moan In My Mouth*." He looked
at me and waited for my feedback. He always did that like my
opinion matters.

"That title makes it sound like it's freaked out the game."

"It is. Watch, this hoe gon' turn out to be a movie one day,
watch. I'on care if I have to save up the money on my own."

I sat up in my bunk. "If it's fire like you say it is, you'll make it
to the big screen. I got faith in yo' work. You just have to have faith
in God and trust the process."

He nodded and stayed silent. "Memphis, I noticed you
sometimes talk about God, but you seem like you astray. Why is
that?"

I chuckled lightly. "Good question. I'on know. I mean, I do. It's
like this with me. I'm from Memphis. My city is fucked up. Nawl,
y'all be thinking Dallas and Houston fucked up; it ain't. Y'all party
a lot. We bury a lot. Y'all got trains and buses; we got black hearse."
I sighed and said, "I used to go to church damn near every Sunday
growing up. But I noticed two things: one, my grandma carried a
.38 revolver with her to church. No lie, that's a big fact. I had to ask
myself, why would she have to carry a gun to church when her God
was supposed to protect her?"

Kingpen thought hard and shrugged.

"Exactly," I said. "Then the pastor made a pass at one of my
aunts. I used to look up to him. Not only that, but he went to prison."

Kingpen laughed. "You goin' hard. Yo' preacher ain't go to
prison."

"If I'm lying, I'm dying."

"What did he go to the pen for?" he asked curiously.

"He burned the church down for the insurance money."

"You're bullshitting."

I shook my head. "No lie. But that didn't make me stop
believing in God, but it did make me stop believing in people. All
that showed me was that people can be devious, conniving, and

downright disloyal. I feel like my grandma probably felt: *Yea, I believe in God, how else did we get here? But, he gave us free will to think on our own*! I'm like my grandma in the world. If God gon' give me free will to think on my own, I'ma think, but if push comes to shove, I'ma let my gun do the talking."

Kingpen laughed. "I got to meet your grandma. I know she's hell."

I smiled as I thought about my black queen. She was a true gangsta. Raising my badass. "Yeah, she's lovely. She's like a rose. Smells good, beautiful, but if you hold her the wrong way she'll make you bleed."

A C.O. walked up to my cell door. "Joshua Curry!" He looked at me briefly, then walked off.

Kingpen jumped in his bunk to give me room to finish getting ready. As I grabbed my toothbrush, I looked at my celly.

"In a few days I'ma give you something to write about in yo' books"

***

"Daddy!" Princess ran to me as soon as I walked through the visitation room.

The visitation room wasn't crowded like I expected. Mainly because you weren't able to get a contact visit without first getting vaccinated for the Corona virus. So many dumb niggas refused to get the two shots, saying that they were injecting chips into our bodies. Dumb ass niggas.

The space tab separated from each table gave me enough room to talk to my family without having to hear the next person's conversation.

I pecked her lips. "There," she smiled as I carried her to our table.

Jessica stood up looking like a lighter version of Jhene Aiko in her red and yellow flower dress. Her hair was in a long ponytail that flowed down her back.

"Hey, baby daddy." She held her arms open like a queen does for a true king.

I flowed into her arms. Princess giggled as I kissed her mom. We were the only ones there. "Eww!" Princess chimed in.

"No tongues, no tongues, eww! Nasty!" Princess giggled.

We broke away from our passionate kiss as we took our seats. Princess sat on my lap as I stared into Jessica's eyes. Every time I saw her, she reminded me of how much I loved her.

"Daddy, me and mommy got your favorite." She held up two bags of Ranch Style Doritos, two sprites, two carrot cakes, and two packs of skittles.

I kissed the top of her head. "You got all of this for me?" She wiggled and squirmed in my arms. "Daddy, stop! That tickles!"

I laughed and stopped. I had people all around the visitor room looking at us and smiling. I knew my little girl was adorable. They didn't have to tell me. I looked over at Jessica; she was all smiles. "What's up, beautiful. What's on your mind?"

She shook her head to avoid the tears. "Nothing, it's just that—"

She sighed.

I reached for her hand. She laid her car keys on the table and I grabbed her hand. "Tell daddy, what's wrong?"

The onslaught of tears invaded her cheeks. She turned her face and tried to wipe them away. It was too late. The floodgates were already open. "Mommy, why are you crying?" Princess asked, then she looked up at me.

Princess jumped out of my lap and walked to Jessica. The whole way, her *Hello Kitty* light-up shoes flashed red. "Mommy, don't cry."

Jessica made my heart melt. I know I was the reason for her tears. I felt it. My heart ached when hers did; we were one. I had abandoned my family when she was only seven months' pregnant. I got jammed up and sent to county jail. I made bond to see Princess born, but once my trial ended, I was sent back to the county. Jessica was just turning eighteen, and I was turning nineteen. She had turned into a grown up overnight. Basically, a single parent.

Jessica wiped her tears. She wasn't ready to face me, and I understood. She picked Princess up and sat her on her lap. Princess played with Jessica's ponytail.

"Jess, look at me," I said softly. Jessica, being stubborn, ignored me. "Jessica, babe, look at me, and tell daddy what's wrong."

She looked at me and huffed. "I fucking miss you, Josh. That's what's wrong. The only time Princess smiles like this, is when we come down here to see you. We both miss you. It's hard without you, Josh."

The thug in me wouldn't let me cry amongst the nosey inmates that surrounded the room. But my heart felt like Mike Tyson was using it for a punching bag. Her words hurt. I knew she loved me. I could feel her love miles away. I also knew I was the cause of her lonely nights. I was the reason she had to take Princess to her first daddy daughter dance.

I lifted my eyes to prevent myself from crying. I sighed and said, "Jess, I'm sorry. I know I say that every time I come down here, but I'm for real. This shit hurts me too. Not a second goes by that I don't think about y'all. Every night, I dream of coming home to y'all. Y'all are the drive I use to get up every morning when I don't feel like getting up. It's moments like these that keeps me from giving up."

Princess stared into my eyes from across the table. "I can't imagine what you go through here day in and day out. I just want you home, we want you home," Jessica said.

"And I'm coming home soon. Trust me and when I do, I'm coming home to my family."

Jessica smirked. "What about these penitentiary thotties you are whispering to in here?"

I laughed. I knew she would bring it up. "Laugh it up, but I'm serious," she said. Princess laughed like she actually knew what was funny. Jessica laughed seeing Princess laugh. "See, you even got your daughter thinking it's funny," she said. And just like that, the waters had calmed.

"Believe me, what I tell these females in here is just a figment of their own imagination. I take the info they give me and create myself into the man of their dream. Even though they mostly know I'm gaming them, they so used to being played that they just accept it, hit the reset button, and hope for a different outcome. The only thing you should worry 'bout, is what place you wanna live in when I come home. 'Cause every dollar I make, will go to your cash app.

"Ohh, mommy. Let's move to Be-at-nom." She pronounced it wrong, making Jessica laugh.

"It's Vietnam—and no, baby, when daddy comes home, he won't be able to leave the country just yet. But, we can go and visit your cousins. You wanna do that?" Princess nodded.

Princess reached across the table, practically climbing on it to get to a canned sprite. "Daddy, help!" she screamed.

I laughed and pulled the soda closer to me. "Not fair, daddy!" She jumped out of Jessica's lap and ran to my lap. I picked her up and kissed both cheeks. She poked her lips out. "You keep forgetting." I smiled and pecked her lips.

I opened her soda and handed it to her. Jessica held an open bag of Doritos across the table to me as she placed a chip in her mouth, winking at me. I looked inside the bag of chips. There was some money that was Saran-wrapped tightly inside. I nodded at her and opened the other bag for Princess.

The rest of the visit went as a blur. Two hours felt like thirty minutes. As we stood up to leave, I felt Jessica getting sad all over again. We hugged. "I hate this place. I don't like leaving you here. If I could stay in a cell with you I would." I grabbed her. I reached my hand under the helm of her dress, and she moaned and slapped my chest.

"You better stop. Starting shit you know you can't finish." She lightly bit my lip.

I looked around for Princess. "Princess!" I called after her. She was sitting in the lap of another inmate as he had a pack of skittles. As soon as I saw her, I saw red.

"What—the—fuck!" I walked in his direction and snatched Princess from his lap. I handed Princess to Jessica. The inmate stood up.

"Bitch ass nigga, the fuck you doing with my daughter in yo' lap!" I spat. I could feel my nerves causing my body to shake.

"Fam, I ain't got to be no bitch. It wasn't even like that. I was just—" I muffed him with my palm before he could let his words out.

"Daddy!" Princess cried.

I looked back at Jessica. "Get my daughter out of here. If I don't call yo' phone tonight, call the unit and see what's up." Jessica nodded and walked away swiftly.

Ol' boy was coming at me. Before he could come face to face with me, another inmate in crisp whites stepped in the middle of us. I looked at him like he could get the business too.

"I ain't tryna be in y'all business, but I'ma let y'all know sum, if y'all pop sum off in here with these free-world people, y'all going under the jail."

"Fuck that, this nigga finna go under the dirt for touching my daughter!" I spat.

"I understand how you feel, homie, but dig this. If you kill him around all those innocent people, you'll never be able to hold yo' daughter again. At least not for another ten years." He placed his hand on my shoulder and led me out the room.

The nigga that was holding my daughter walked past us. "This ain't over," he said, trying to save face.

"All you gotta do is say what wing you on, and I'm pulling up!"

"I'm on J-Wing," he said. "You better ask niggas about Turk," Turk said.

"Fuck askin' about you. You can't ask about me 'cause I'on leave no witnesses. I'ma see you, playboy. Fasho!"

"Chill, homie. Don't showcase yo' spit boxing game. Just pull up on him and handle your business."

I nodded. I was out of character for that. But that nigga Turk had me heated. Nigga should never touch my seed. In no shape, form, or fashion; that's an automatic death sentence.

"Preciate you, family." I dap'd him up. "Memphis," I introduced myself.

"Vetta Vucci," he said.

We walked to the cage to get stripped out. I took my shirt off; Vucci looked at me. "You a homie?" He noticed the red five point stars tat'd on my neck and chest.

"I'm a vice lord."

"Oh, so you people—" He held his hand out like Eastwood had showed me. We shook up. "I'ma blood. I'm from Fortworth. If you need anything, let me know. I take care of mines, and now that we're family, don't even worry 'bout that nigga, Turk. I'll get it handled."

"I appreciate it, Vetta Vucci, but that shit is personal with me. He touched my daughter. That's my seed, feel me? I got to handle that."

Vucci nodded. "I can respect that. But he is a known disciple on the unit. He got a lil' clout. So just to be on the safe side, when you finally decide to handle yo' business, shoot me a kite, I'll fall over there with you. Ask about me, I'ma through bred street nigga. For real!"

I nodded. What I was planning on doing to Turk, I wanted no witness around, but I kept that to myself.

"Preciate it, family." I leaned a little closer and spoke above a whisper. "I just *sco'd.* Later, I'ma have a few whips and some gas for sale. Pull up on me." That was the plan. To wait until I came from visitation to act like I had scored from visit, so niggas wouldn't know exactly where I'd got the real pack from.

Vetta Vucci nodded. "Overstood. You say yo' name Memphis, right."

I nodded. "The one and only!"

Chapter Fifteen

Newton

Knock! Knock! Knock!

"Mommy, someone's at the doo-oo!" Jacob yelled from the living room.

I wiped my hand on the dish towel as I set the timer on the stove. I had just finished making me and Jacob a dish of my homemade lasagna; it was Jacob's favorite dish. He loved the way I used different cheeses on the three different layers. On one layer, I used cheddar cheese on the ground meat. On the second layer I used Mozzarella cheese and bacon strips. And the third layer I used nacho cheese and chopped turkey bites. Jacob could never get enough of the lasagna. He would have me make it at least once a month for him.

Knock! Knock! Knock! The visitor knocked again.

"I'm coming!" I shouted as I limped to the front door.

I opened the door and had a surprised look at the visitor.

"McFee. How may I help you?"

McFee stood on the opposite side of the door in a pair of tan khakis and an army fatigue cool shit. He had gained a lot of weight since the last time I saw him. His belly was hanging over his belt.

"Hi, nice to see you, Ms. Newton," he said as his played with his hands.

"Likewise, I guess," I said as I stood at the door.

"Uhm, do you mind if I come in, Ms. Newton?" he asked.

"I really do."

He sighed. "I deserve that. I know how you feel. But I want to make amends with you, if you'll just give me the opportunity."

"McFee, what's this really about? I know you didn't drive all the way to my house just to apologize. You are my friend on Facebook. You could've easily sent me a direct message"

"I know. But this, I thought, should be discussed in person. It's about Gianni."

As he said Gianni's name, my suspicion of what he was really here for kicked in. My curiosity gave in. "Jacob, go to your room for a minute, baby."

"Aw, ma. I'm working on getting this new level," Jacob said as he played his video game.

Jacob sighed and paused the game. He reluctantly stomped to his room. I stepped to the side as McFee walked in the house. I closed the door behind him. "Can I get you anything to drink?"

He sucked his gut in just to stuff his hand in his pocket. "Water would be fine."

I limped in the kitchen and grabbed a bottle of Fiji water from the fridge. I walked back in the room. McFee was looking at the bottle after I handed it to him and led him to the couch. I placed Jacob's controller on the table and sat down.

"How's he taking everything?" I knew he was asking about Jacob.

"He's taking it one day at a time. He's seeing a psychiatrist once a week. It's somewhat helping," I said.

"I see you still have pictures of Mr. Kiles around, that's good."

"Seth's Jacob's father. No matter what happened, I still try to feed Jacob's mind with the positive things Seth did for his family." I stopped briefly and continued. "I thought you said you had something to say about Gianni."

McFee took a gulp from the water and said, "I do. I-uh—last night I was at home in bed. My motion sensor lights keep going off around my house, I have rodents running around all night eating from my wife's garden, so I didn't think too much of it. That was until they kept going off. Something told me to look out the window, so I did. When I raised the blinds, I saw him."

"Saw who?"

"Gianni Kingsley."

I lightly chuckled. "You're kidding, right?" I asked. "We both know he's dead."

McFee sat on the edge of the couch. "I know that. That's what's bothering me, because I saw him, like I'm seeing you. But he was gone, just like that." He snapped his fingers.

"If you want, I can give you the number to Jacob's psychiatrist.

"I'm not crazy, Newton. I'm not. I know what I saw."

"But you also saw him die. So?"

"I know. But—" he started whispering. "What if he didn't die? What if he's very much alive?"

I started laughing nervously. "McFee, you need some help. Mental help."

He shook his head. "Maybe you're right. It's just crazy. Why does he want to haunt me? Out of all the people his ghost haunts me."

I laughed. "Well, you did give him hell when he was alive."

McFee laughed. "I know." He patted his leg and stood up. "I'm sorry to bother you, Ms. Newton. I just felt that I should talk to someone, and I'm glad I talked to you."

I led him to the door. "The only reason he's haunting you is because you won't let go. You have to let that entire day go. We all lost a lot that day."

"How do you get by day by day without thinking about what happened?" he asked.

"I think about it, but I think about how Gianni rescued me without trying, that's how I get by. And I stay busy raising Jacob."

McFee smiled and nodded. "If you ever need someone to talk to, I'll always respond on Facebook."

I nodded. "I'll be fine." I opened the door as he stepped into the sun. "Take care." He nodded and walked to his truck.

As soon as I slammed the door, Jacob ran back into the room and started playing his video game. I picked up my iPhone and dialed a number.

"Hello!" Gianni answered.

"We need to talk."

"What's up?" he asked.

"He knows."

"Who?"

"McFee," I said.

Gianni laughed. "I'll be at home in an hour. I'm about to get off work in like thirty minutes."

"Okay. I'll come over." I hung up.

I sat my phone down and sighed. I thought back to how I found out Gianni Kingsley was not in fact dead, but very much alive—

Ding-Ding! Ding-Ding! The doorbell rang as I rose up off the couch to get the door. As I opened the door, no one stood on the opposite side waiting for me. I stepped out the door and looked around, no one was there, not even an unknown car. I looked down and there was a gift box wrapped with a blue bow on it. I picked the box up and looked around again.

I shrugged and stepped back inside the house.

"What's that, mommy?"

"Let's find out." Jacob stood beside me as I untied the blue box. I ripped the nice gift wrap off and opened the box. There was a letter inside with a sonogram. The sonogram was of Gianni's and Stephanie's unborn son, Gianni the third. I picked the letter up and started from the beginning:

Gabby,

I hope all is well with you and your gangsta son, Jacob. I know you're probably wondering who this is. First and foremost, don't have a heart attack. But it's me, yes, me, as in GK. I know it seems unreal. I know you're probably thinking someone's playing a horrible joke on you, but it's the truth. I didn't want to put much detail into this letter just in case it got in the wrong hands, but I'll explain it to you more in person. Come see me. This is my address 3412 Pine Lake, Longview, Texas 75601. Hope to see you soon.

Love Always,

G.K.

I teared up as I looked at the letter. It couldn't be. I knew this had to be some sick joke. It had to be. Gianni Kingsley was dead. I watched him die. He got shot multiple times. I watched as blood dripped from the corner of his mouth.

"Mommy, what was that?" Jacob asked. I wiped my tears and jumped up with a letter in my hand.

"Jacob, get dressed, we're going somewhere!" I looked around for my keys and purse. I grabbed my .380 from the top shelf, just in case. Ever since the incident, I started taking classes on how to properly shoot a gun for my safety, and Jacob's.

"Where we going?" Jacob asked as he ran into the living room with his shoes on and his portable video game.

I opened the door and locked it behind us. "Get in the car, you'll see when we get there." I put a little pep in my step as I jumped behind the wheel. I know I did eighty on a sixty-five-mile limit. I was anxious. Nervous, even excited.

As I made the drive, I wondered if Gianni could've pulled it off. I never put anything past him. He was invincible. My mind started playing tricks on me. I had thoughts of him alive, smiling. Then the thought would get repealed with the images of him dying as his head laid on Stephanie's lap.

Please Lord, let him be alive, I silently prayed because if he was, and he played dead, I am going to kill him myself.

As I pulled up to the address I was given, I looked at the letter one last time as I folded it up and grabbed my purse.

"Jacob, don't let no one in the car, and don't leave until I come for you." Jacob nodded as he continued to play his game.

I stepped out of the car and walked up the steps. The wooden steps creaked under my foot. The front door had an oval shaped glass in the middle. A thick colored curtain hung behind the glass. I knocked three times and waited. Before long, two little girls ran to the door. I couldn't tell the difference between them. They smiled and ran away. Stephanie walked up to the door. She opened it and smiled. I handed her the letter without saying a word. She read it and smiled.

"It's about time he told you." She looked over her shoulder and yelled. "Gianni, someone's at the door for you."

My heart raced as I looked at her, wondering if this was all a horrible joke. I got my answer as Gianni walked towards Stephanie. He looked at me and smiled. It was him. Gianni Kingsley. The man that I had fell in love with while working in a prison. The man that stole my heat and has yet to return it. The man that saved my life, without ever trying. He was here. Right in front of me. Breathing the same air as me, but how? I thought to myself: When I watched him die, I watched him take his last breath.

He gave me his sinister smile and said, "Aren't you going to say something?"

My mouth opened to speak but no words came out. I got lightheaded as my heart rose. My knees felt weak. And I collapsed.

Chapter Sixteen

Hotboy

I hung the phone after calling Stephanie to inform her that Gabby would be coming over. I had just got off of work. My first day actually. I got hired and was asked to start immediately. I worked for human waste management for TDCJ. My first day was cool. We picked up the trash at the Michales Unit, then the Coffield Unit. I was hoping we would pick up the trash at Beto so that I could put my plan into action. But soon. I just had to have patience. It was crazy, because I did all of those calendar years in the pen, and still struggled with patience.

As I got home, I walked in the house and locked the door. "Bae, is that you?" Steph asked as she walked in the room. She wore a pair of pink soccer shorts that made her legs look toned and desirable.

"Yeah, I just got off." I kissed her lips.

"How was it?"

"Different! I actually felt good. Knowing I was working for the state, and I'm getting paid to do it." I laughed as I thought back to how I used to work on the Beto sign plant for free, while they made millions a year.

"Are you hungry?" Steph asked as she walked in the kitchen. I watched her ass move in her shorts the whole way. *Damn! Bae still got it. Ol' lil booty ass*! I thought to myself as I followed behind her to the kitchen.

"Yea, I'm hungry," I said as she walked to the kitchen sink.

"What are you hungry for?" she asked. "I went to the grocery store earlier, me and the twins. I bought ground meat, taco shells, burger buns, tortilla chips and nacho cheese. I can cook tacos, hamburgers, or Rotele dip."

I walked behind her and planted my dick on her ass. "I'm hungry for you." I rubbed my dick all over her lil' booty. She moaned and tilted her head to the side, giving me full access to her hotspot. I kissed her neck and trailed my tongue behind her ears.

"Where's the twins?" I asked as she reached behind me to grab a hold of my dick.

"They're asleep. It's their naptime." She faced me and stuck her hand in my pants. Her small hand gripped my dick.

I stopped her and said: "Wait, let me take a shower first."

"Let's take one together!" she said as she grabbed my hand and led me to the bathroom.

I stopped and checked in on the twins as Steph kept going to the bathroom. I could hear the shower water turn on as I stuck my head in the twins' room. They were both stretched out on their separate beds asleep. I smiled and closed the door back. I couldn't wait to add onto the family with my little nigga on the way.

As I made it to the bathroom, Stephanie was already naked under the water. I stared at her petite body as I stepped out of my clothes. I stepped under the water behind her. She grabbed my body wash and some towels. I turned my back to her as she began to wash my body. She washed my back, then my shoulders. The *Dove Men Care* body wash invaded the shower, sending a fresh scent in the air. I turned and faced her; she started washing my chest as she made her way down my abs.

"I love you, Gianni," she said as I leaned down to taste her lips. The shower water made her hair look slick. She washed my dick off with the towel as I swallowed her lips in mine.

The towel fell to the bottom of the tub. I grabbed her by her small waist and picked her up. Her body weight came down as she guided my dick into her tight hole from behind.

"Mmhuh! Yes! Now, daddy's home!" she crooned in my ear.

The water warmed my head as her pussy warmed my other head. She rode my dick standing up as I held on to her ass.

"I love this pussy, bae!" I said as I lightly bit her neck and began to suck on it.

"Sh-Show me!" she moaned. "B-beat it up!" she said.

I slammed her back against the wall and gripped her legs under my arms. Her pussy spread as her juicy pink lips sucked my dick inside of her hole. I pounded her pussy as I held her up with a tight grip.

"That's it, daddy, give me my dick. Ahh, fuck! Yes!" she yelled. She clawed at my shoulders. I smelled her back against the other shower wall. She moaned as she breathed into my mouth.

"Uh! Yes! Stroke my pussy! Just—like—that!"

I gripped under her soft ass as I drilled into her pussy. I was drilling in her like I was looking for oil. She kissed my lips as our tongues made love. I can't lie, she had some of the best pussy I've ever had. Plus, she was pregnant with our son, so her pussy was very wet.

"I'm close, bae, I can feel it," she whispered.

"Me, too!" I grunted as I kept stroking her pussy.

"Faster!" she demanded.

I jackhammered her pussy as I felt my nut building. I had her bent up like a pretzel in my arms as she cried out and moaned my name. "Gi-an-ii!" She came all over my dick as I shot my seed inside of her.

She breathed into my mouth as I held her up with the help of the shower wall. I slowly let her down as the euphoric feeling slowly faded away. She looked at me and sank to her knees. She grabbed my semi-erect dick in her hand. Her touch sent tingles up my body as her tongue kissed the head. The sensitive feeling had me shaking like a leaf in the wind.

Steph took my dick all the way in her mouth as she moved her head from side to side. "You're mine," she moaned with my dick in her mouth,

I held myself up with the help of the shower walls as I closed my eyes and said, "Damn! I love the fuck out of you, gurl!"

After our showers, Steph started cooking us some tacos. I woke the girls up and put their favorite movie, *Sparkle*, on. They watched that movie over twenty times.

A knock came at the door. I figured it had to either be Lakewood or Gabby because they were the only two people who knew where we stayed. I opened the door, and Gabby smiled at me. Jacob briefly looked up from his portable game.

"Y'all just in time. Stephanie's making tacos." I stepped to the side to let them in.

"Oh, tacos! I love tacos!" Jacob said as he ran in the living room.

During the course of Gabby finding out I wasn't dead, her and Stephanie spent quite a bit of time together, which meant Jacob spent a lot of time with the twins. He liked it though, being that he was the only child; he treats the twins as if they're his blood sisters. And they enjoyed it, too.

I closed the door and followed Gabby to the kitchen where Stephanie was throwing down. The seasoned ground meat had the whole house smelling good. She had soft taco shells and hard shells already laid out ready to be warmed.

"Hey, Gabby!" Stephanie greeted her. Gabby walked behind her and hugged her from the back while Stephanie tended to the food.

"It smells good here. Do you need any help?" Gabby asked.

"Uhm, yes! If you can, dice up two or three tomatoes. That'll help. I basically got everything else ready."

I sat on the barstool as I watched the two of them interact like they were best friends. Over the past few weeks, they practically became best friends. Other than the love for me, I didn't know what they had in common. I didn't ask either. Just let them do them. I was just happy that they were getting along. I had always told Stephanie that no matter what, I would stay in touch with Gabby. I didn't love Gabby like I once did, but I would always love her. She did carry my seed at one point in time. And Stephanie respected me more for that.

After Gabby finished washing her hands, she grabbed the tomatoes, a cutting knife and board, and started cutting the tomatoes.

"So, McFee came by my house today," Gabby said.

Stephanie looked at her, puzzled. "Really why?"

I sat on the stool, trying my best not to laugh. "Ask him." Gabby straight snitched me out.

Stephanie placed her right hand on the sink and sighed.

"Gianni, what did you do?" she asked.

I grabbed a few pieces of diced tomatoes and laughed. I tossed them in my mouth and said, "Nothing."

"He scared McFee, standing outside his window the other night." Gabby recapped the entire story to Steph word for word. Once she finished, Stephanie looked at me like she wanted to kill me.

"Why, Gianni? Do you want to go back to prison?" Steph asked.

"I'm never going back. They'll have to kill me first."

"And you think they won't! You're supposed to be dead. Do you know what that means? That means, if they find out you're not, they'll kill you to save face!" Stephanie said.

"Sure will!" Gabby agreed with her.

That was one thing I hated. With it just being me and Jacob, we were outnumbered with the women, two to one. We never got a fair trial, ever!

"I got this. I know what I'm doing," I tried to reason.

"If you called him, how in the hell did he even see you?" Stephanie asked. She laid the shells onto an oven pan and stuck the item in the oven. I was glad, too. The sooner we eat, the sooner they can both shut the hell up.

"That was exactly what I wanted. I wanted the fat pig to see me."

"Then what?" Steph asked.

Gabby laughed and said, "I have to be honest; he was scared. When he came to my house, he was jittery. The way he kept talking about you it was like he had seen a ghost."

I laughed. "That's not funny, Gianni! You're playing with fire," Steph said.

"I got this. Just trust me."

"So, what's your plan?" Gabby asked.

"To make his life a living hell. Once I'm done with him, he'll wish he was dead!"

Chapter Seventeen

Memphis

A Week Later

Time had really started to fly for me. Money was hitting Jessica's cash app like we had won a settlement. She was happy, too. She had started pulling up more now that she had money to travel back and forth. Eastwood was doing his best shit; he had started selling his shares for seven hundred, until he saw I was boomin' mines for four. He then took his price down to five hundred. The Jags, I had got off of them bitches quickly. I sold some to a few niggas that sco'd from me. Gave them a playa deal. I sold one jag' with the charger for thirteen hundred. Then I sold the other three phones to another nigga for a reasonable price, without the chargers.

Through all of the hustling, I made a small name for myself. No matter how bad I tried to keep it under wraps, niggas would still scream my name, saying that I had the cheapest prices on Beto. At first I was worried that the wrong person would hear and the heat would come down on me. But, I made sure to always keep my cell clear of all contraband, and to never pull out the Jag' until I was sure Lieutenant McFee was not on the unit. I hadn't had an encounter with the infamous mall cop and I was tryna keep it that way. Big Tank had pulled a few strings and got me a job on the wing as the third shift porter. During the day when the cool rank was here, I would work the hallways, pushing the officers juice cart up and down the hallway. I had made a lot of so-called friends, being that I had the dope. But, being that I was pumping my shit so cheap, I was down to my last fifty sheets. And since I didn't have a mule, I would be back at square one. So, I had to do what I did best. Break a bitch!

"Eat, lil' nigga, you got it!" I encouraged my workout partner, Lil Swole. Lil Swole was a disciple from Houston. Even though I was a vice lord and he was a folk, we still cliqued tight like LeBron and Anthony Davis, me being LeBron.

Swole stood up. His chest was poking out like a double chin. "Damn, my nigga, you be pushing me to the limit." His voice sounded dry as his chest heaved up and down.

I hit the floor to do my set. I did my pushups with ease. I've been doing them for so long, that it felt normal to my muscles. Like I wasn't even working out. I stood up barely sweating.

"What did you want to do on that game tonight?" Lil Swole asked me as I held my hands over my head.

"Yo' talkin' 'bout Tennessee and Houston?"

He nodded. "Yeah. Make it light on yo'self."

I laughed. Me and Swole would damn near bet on every game, especially if Houston and Tennessee were playing. We would bet anything from fifty to a hundred dollars a game. We called that *something light*, just to make the game interesting.

"Bet a dollar," I said, taking the Tennessee Titans. He knew I was a die-hard Titans fan. But you couldn't tell Swole shit. He was so Houston.

"That's a bet. Don't trip out, shit that, grip out!" he said, then laughed.

I looked at my watch. It was close to a shift change. I snatched my shower bag up and dap'd Swole up. "I gotta take a shower. When I win, you know the app name, shoot my duckets!" I joked.

He laughed as I walked out the dayroom. As I put my state shirt on, I waited at the gate. They were already doing shift change. A redhead white girl walked by the gate. She was still on OJT status. She nodded at me as she walked by.

I shook my head. It was my favorite time of year. Thot season!

"D-Wing boss!" I yelled for the C.O. "You want some juice or water? A short chubby, wide booty African American C.O. walked up to the door. The way she walked, it looked as if she was walking on the side of her foot. It looked as if it hurt, but she was smiling instead of frowning.

"Uhm, let me get two cups of ice, please." Her accent sounded different like she wasn't from Texas. I read her name on her name tag: *Ravens.*

I lifted the cooler lid and filled two Styrofoam cups up with ice. I placed both cups of ice on the D-Wing gate.

"Thank you, Memphis." She caught me by surprise.

I looked at her in shock. "How do you know my name?" She scooped a piece of ice in her mouth with her tongue. She swished the cold piece of ice around in her mouth and said: "Boy, er'body know your name."

I laughed at her accent. "Where are you from, Ms. Raven?"

"I'm from B-More. Baltimore all day!" She repped her hometown. As I looked at her, I wondered if every chick from Baltimore had the same button nose like she had. She had the same kind of nose that Cindy had from the movie, *The Grinch*.

One of my homies named Hood walked up to the gate. "What's poppin', bitch? Let me get a cup of juice." Hood was a bald head brown-skinned cat. He resembled the retired basketball player, Big Baby Davis. Hood was a Piru from Longview, Texas. He was incarcerated for smoking some dude for touching his daughter. I had the utmost respect for him pushing a nigga wig back for touching his seed. Because as soon as I caught that nigga Turk, I was gon' do the same thing.

I filled Hood's *Cowboys* cup up with some watered down juice. "That shit will fuck yo' kidneys up," I said as I handed his cup back.

"What, this juice?" he asked as he gulped half the cup. I shook my head. "Nawl, that Cowboys star," I joked back, laughing.

"Fuck you!" he laughed.

I chucked the deuces and pushed the cart down the hall. "What about me, I'on get none?" It was the same redhead chick that I saw during shift change. I didn't know her name, but everyone called her Skittles.

I'on know why they called her Skittles, 'cause she definitely didn't look like she tasted good. Now, if you would've called her sour skittles, I'd understand. Don't get me wrong, she wasn't ugly, but she wasn't pretty. She wore loose blue khaki pants, a pair of Adidas, and a black kill guard. A kill guard was a black overcoat that the majority of the bad built C.O.'s rocked to hide their gut. Her lips were flushed purple. Every time I saw her, she was snacking on something.

"You want something to drink?" I asked.

"Nah, I was just joking." She smiled at me as she sat in the A, B, C, D picket on the stairs.

"So, what's up? How you like the unit so far?" I asked.

"It's cool. I really wish they would let me work the north side." She looked down the hall as she said it. I already knew her reason. I had heard rumors of her liking a few cats on the unit. I wasn't hatin' though; I was actually happy. I was a hundred percent for the game. To me if another inmate won a C.O., trained them the convict way, we all win. Not that I was looking for a handout, but as long as there was dope flowing through the unit, then there would be a product for me to buy.

"What, you don't like the suburbs anymore?" I asked. A lot of C.O.'s and inmates considered the south side of the unit the suburbs. Privileged living. Like the grass was greener on this side. In a sense, it was. Because the north end rarely has females.

"It ain't that." She sighed.

"You can't compare the wings until you came to the hotel," I said, referring to the H-Wing. We had given H-wing the nickname, Hotel because that's how we ran it. Whenever a female C.O. worked H-Wing, we made their stay lovely.

"I haven't worked over there yet. I heard y'all are not so bad." She gave me a half smile.

"Not so bad," I said. "It's lovely. And guess what makes it so live?"

"What?" she asked with one eyebrow raised.

"I'm over there."

She smiled. "Stop it!" She looked at my appearance. I knew she was checking me out. I always kept myself looking like I was going to the prom.

My shag dropped waves like the ocean. I had waves inside my waves; my shit was hitting so hard. My whites stayed cocaine and crisped. My shoes didn't have a spot or scuff on them. My Cartiers shined like the sun as the gold resembled a mirror for whoever was staring in my eyes.

Skittles nodded. I knew without work that I had won her approval. I knew she'd added me to her list. Now all I had to do was make it to the number one spot.

"You think you're fly, don't you?" She blushed. Openly, I said: Nawl, I'on think I'm fly. I'm just me."

She nodded. "So, why are you a con artist?"

I laughed. "I wouldn't say that. I'm a finesser, a persuader."

She nodded.

"Prove it!" She hooked the bait on the line and swung it into the lake. Instead of me being a greedy fish, I let the bait sit there to show her that I had discipline.

"Let me make my rounds, I'll be back."

Chapter Eighteen

Anastasia

"Oh my God! Would you please rack the hell up!" I yelled at a group of inmates as I tried to get L-Wing under control.

Every time I would rack them up, they would somehow pop back out of their cell. And I was getting sick and tired chasing them around. I tried to come to work and be a cool C.O., and not treat them like other C.O.'s treated them, but they were taking my kindness for a weakness.

As I went up the back half of the stairs to get to two rows, the inmates that I was chasing ran down the front half. My pants were so tight I couldn't run, and as pretty as I looked, I wasn't trying to. To chase behind them would cause me to sweat. Sweating would loosen up my braids. And I had just got them done the day before, so that was not gon' happen.

"Bro, would ya'll—" I huffed. "You know what? Fuck this shit!" I walked down the stairs and walked up to the gate.

"L-Wing out!" I yelled.

I saw the female keyboss, who I nicknamed Baby Teeth, because all of her front teeth were small. Baby Teeth walked up to the gate. She was African or Nigerian. Hell, they all looked the same. She had a low, dirty blonde curl-type fro. She had been on Beto maybe six months before me, so she felt that she had power over me. We had been beefing all day, and it was apparent she didn't like me. Really, she was just another hater.

Get in line, bitch, I thought to myself.

"You have to rack them up first, before I can let you off the wing," Baby Teeth said.

"I did, but they keep coming back out. Can you open the gate?" I said as I tried to keep my cool.

"Ms. Davenport, I can't. Wait until you secure your wings," she said with a smirk on her face.

I instantly got upset. "You need to secure some bigger teeth, now open the motherfucking gate!" I yelled. So much for keeping my cool. Other inmates and cops stopped and watched from the hallway. I didn't give two fucks. I was tryna keep my cool. But if they wanted to see a bitch act an ass, I was going to show them how an East Texas bitch acts an ass.

Baby Teeth turned to one of her Nigerian co-workers as they started to align in their native tongue. Baby Teeth pointed at me as she talked. She had this dumbass smile on her face. That shit had me hotter than pork chop grease.

"Bitch, if you got som' to say, then say it now!" Baby Teeth smiled, but she did it walking backwards to a safe distance.

"Davenport!" My homegirl BoBo grabbed me. BoBo was African too. But she didn't act nothing like them. BoBo was cool. Super cool and laid back. She was tall, like six foot four. She was skinny though, with micro braids. She loved basketball. Her favorite player was LeBron James; that's all she ever talked about. LeBron James this, LeBron James that. She watched all of his games and could tell you all of his stats.

"What, BoBo!" I shouted as she pulled me down the hall out of earshot. The sergeant stood beside her. I was so mad, that tears had started falling down my face. I was one of those emotional fighters. Once you got me really upset, I would go so much into a rage, that I would start crying.

"D, you can't be acting like that at work. Come on, sis', you know better than that." BoBo laughed. She knew that bitch had some little ass teeth.

"Leave her alone, that's not nice." BoBo laughed again. The sergeant tried to talk to me, but I was only half listening. I knew he was just tryna be on my good side 'cause BoBo was around. "Don't be letting those people see you cry out here like this."

I laughed and looked towards the south end of the unit. Before I could wipe my face, I locked eyes with an inmate that I've been having constant dreams about. I knew he saw the tears, but I still turned my head to try to hide my emotional state from him

He turned the officers' juice cart around and went the other way. There he was, going back to the suburbs, while I was stuck in the projects with Baby Teeth.

***

Memphis

Seeing the tears run down Davenport's face did something to me. I can't lie, I was a sucker for women in tears. I felt that women were too precious to cry. Seeing the tears run down her face made me want to swoop down and save her. Call me a captain save-a-hoe, I don't care.

To prevent myself from getting upset, I turned the juice cart around and went back to the southside. A short distance later, I parked the cart and headed towards the A, B, C, D block. I still had some unfinished business left.

"Memphis!" Ms. Raven called my name. She was leaning on the gate. Her beach ball booty was poking out. Inmates stood behind her in awe as she gave them a full view of her ass.

"Where the ice at? I need some more." She smiled, displaying her pearly white teeth.

"I sat it in front of the chow hall to get a refill. I got'cha as soon as they refill it."

She smiled and said, "I'ma need two more cups, I seemed to have lost mine."

I smiled. "I got'cha." She nodded and walked off; her ass was all over the place. Her ass had swallowed up her panties.

I shook my head to get the sight out of my mind. I walked up to Skittles. "So, where were we?" she asked.

"Before I start, I have a message for you," I said. She sat up straight on the stairs. "Who is it from?"

"This dude," I said.

"C.O., or inmate?"

"Inmate."

She nodded and said, "Which wing? G-Wing?" I shook my head.

"Nope, he's on the northside."

"K-Kilo?" she said. I shook my head. "M-Mary?" I shook my head again. "O-Oscar?" she said. I nodded.

"Oh, I know who that is. He doesn't want anything," she said.

I was shocked but I didn't let her see it. She had basically given herself up, letting me know what wings she somewhat had a potential boyfriend on. She looked innocent, but I knew right then and there, she was a THOT.

I leaned against the picket and said. "What's your name?"

"My name is Scraggly, but everyone calls me Skittles." She showed me all thirty-two of her teeth.

"I'm not everyone. So, I'm not gon' call you what everyone else calls you."

"Well, what are you going to call me?" she asked.

I gave it a quick thought. "Big head," I said.

"Big head, uh-uh."

"Why not? You got a big ass head."

"I guess."

"You remember earlier, I told you I was a finesser, right?" She nodded. "I want you to know, nobody on O-Wing told me to tell you anything. I made it all up."

She looked at me confused. "Why would you do that?"

"Because what I did was let you snitch on yourself. All you did was tell me which wings you like a different dude on."

That's not finessin'," she said.

"How not?"

"Because—" She had nothing else to say,

"For future reference, whenever another nigga say he got a message for you from another inmate, deny everything. Don't snitch on yourself, feel me?" I was training her for when she finally became my hoe. She had already chose up, now it was up to me to accept her application.

She nodded. "What's your name?"

"Memphis. The one and only."

Chapter Nineteen

Eastwood

Shit was looking good for me. Over the past week, I had a little over fifteen racks. I was having my money sent to Memphis baby mama Jessica Cashapp. I kept tabs in my journal of how much she had. I was tryna stack up at least twenty-five G's to pay for a good appeal lawyer. I wasn't hustling for nothing. I was hustlin' for a purpose.

Today we got blessed with a live second shift, so I decided to duck-off in the cell for a while and check my Facebook account. I logged on and went to Facebook messenger. I had a few friends online. I scrolled through my friends list and noticed Chaz—an ex-C.O.—was online. I clicked on her page to be nosey. She looked different in her free world clothes. Chaz was super skinny, brown-skinned; she always had her hair done. I considered her a baby because of her age. That was until she up'd and had a baby. The whole unit was shocked that her young ass was having a baby. Once she popped her baby out, the baby didn't leave any fat behind. Chaz used to always say: "Little booties matter." And I couldn't agree with her more, 'cause over time, her lil' booty ass had started looking like something. I just knew her pussy is so tight, if I was to put my dick in her lil' pussy, it'll push my shit right back out.

After looking at her pictures, I scrolled back down my friends list. I saw that Hotboy's old Facebook account was online. "But how?" I asked myself.

I clicked on his messenger and sent a dry message.

Me: *If only you were alive to read this. I miss you, homie, I'ma keep up alive.* I pressed *send.*

I looked at the screen and shed a tear. I really missed my lil' homie. If only he could see me now. A grey cloud popped up on his message, indicating that a reply was being typed.

What the fuck! I thought to myself.

HB: *They are screaming Tupac back*!

I laughed as I read the message. But I was really upset that someone was playing on my lil' nigga page.

Me: *Who is this on my nigga page?*

HB: *It's me, snitches!*

I laughed again.

HB: *Damn Eastwood homie, you putting shit on my grave and I ain't even dead.*

I read the message. It took me by surprise. "How the fuck did they know me by Eastwood?" I asked myself.

Me: *Whoever this is, call me 214-772-5555.*

I logged off and waited. A thought came to me that it was probably that chick Grain that Hotboy had been fucking with before he got killed. But then again, I'on think she'll play like this. Then I thought it was Lakewood. He was known for playing a lot.

My phone vibrated. I looked at the screen. The area code was a 903. I peeped out of my cell with my spy mirror. Seeing that the run was cleared, I answered the phone.

***

Hotboy

After Eastwood first messaged me, I started to message him back. My conscience told me not to, but the kid in me made me do it. I missed my nigga and I know he missed me, too. For weeks I wanted to reach out to him, but I felt like McFee was probably watching his mail. So, I didn't. I really fucked up when I logged on to my Facebook account. I would usually make my messenger invisible so no one would see that I was online, but this time I really forgot. When Eastwood told me to call his number, I felt proud. My nigga had finally come up.

I hesitantly dialed his number. I was at home, ducked off in the garage while Gabby and Steph stayed inside, chatting.

Eastwood picked up on the first ring. "Bruh, who is this, playing like my potna Hotboy!" Eastwood spoke into the phone.

I hesitated, thinking if I should just hang up and block his number, or tell him the truth to help him sleep at night.

Fuck it! I thought to myself

"What's good, bitch?"

Eastwood stayed silent. I wish I could've seen his reaction to my voice. I know the look would've been priceless.

"Can't be," Eastwood said. "Say something else."

I laughed. "You remember you grabbed the pack out of my locker and smelt it, thinking it came from a bitch pussy, but really—" He laughed before I could finish.

"Bitch ass nigga, they said you were dead! What—how, bruh? What's really good?"

I laughed. "Everyone thinks I'm dead! The whole world does. Except Gabby, Steph, and Lakewood and now you."

"Who's Steph?" he asked.

"Oh, you know by Grain. Y'all the only ones," I explained.

"But how?"

I recapped the whole story, all the way from when I faked like I couldn't breathe in the O.I.G's office. Ten minutes later after telling the story, he was still in shock.

"Damn, bitch, that's live! So, what, where are you at now? Mexico or som'?

I laughed. "Nawl, I'm in Longview. Me and Steph got a whole kid on the way."

"Longview, what the fuck! You tryna come back to prison or what? That's too close to Beto. You are throwing rocks at the pen!" he said.

"I couldn't leave without my family."

"My nigga, I got at least thirteen mo' years to do before I even see parole, let alone if the hoes let me make it."

"That's why I made a plan to get you out."

Eastwood laughed. "Bruh, you talking crazy. For one how my fat ass gon' run once they hoes get to chasing us."

"You ain't gonna have to run. I got a perfect plan. Look, I work that TDCJ waste management. For the next few weeks all I want you to do is stack, I'ma provide all of the work. The main thing is to stay out of lock up. Don't go to seg'. Pay somebody to get the dope off for you. Stack the bread, so once I get you out, we'll have enough paper saved up. We can really get to Mexico. 'Cause they're going to be looking for you."

"Overstood. Is that it?" Eastwood asked.

"Nawl. I'ma need you to get a job in the sign shop."

"Say no mo'. But, explain to me how you gon' get me out. 'Cause once I get off the phone with you, I'ma start practicing on my Spanish."

I laughed and said, "Peep game. This is how we gon' do it."

Chapter Twenty

Jessica

"How are you feeling, baby girl?" I asked Princess as I sat on the edge of her bed. For the past three days her temperature had been high. I wanted to take her to the hospital, but I was told when I called that it's safer to not bring her in considering the hospital carried so many positive corona virus cases. So, I stayed at home nursing her back to health. Being that Josh was providing the income for us, I was able to call in and miss a few days of work.

"I feel better, mommy." She sat up in her bed. I felt her forehead. It was warm.

"You sure?" I asked.

She nodded. "Uh-huh."

"Do you want to go to gymnastics, or do you want to rest another day?"

She jumped up. "Do I!" she smiled, and jumped up and down on the bed.

I wondered if she really felt better, or if she was just pretending so she could go to gymnastics. I gave her the benefit of the doubt. "Go brush your teeth and wash your face."

"Rarr!" She roared her stinky breath in my face. "Dragon breath rarr!" She laughed.

"Gurl, get your tail and go!" I laughed. She is something else.

As Princess was getting ready, I started packing her gym bag—extra towels, a few packs of Cheese Nips, and some grape juices. A few snacks for her and her friends to snack on while they were there.

"Ready, ma," she said as she ran back in the room. Her eyes looked heavy. I walked up to her and felt her forehead. "I'm okay, mama," she said. I sighed, hoping she really was.

***

Princess stood in line as she waited to get on the high beam. She was anxious about missing the last few days of practice. Princess stood in line dressed in her tights, with her pink tutu over it. She never rehearsed without her tutu.

"Good, Sandy!" Her coach, Coach Brooks, applauded the little girl that was on the high beam.

"Next!" Coach Brooks said. She smiled at Princess. "Good to have you back, Princess. You look stunning, Diva."

"Thank my mama." Princess made Ms. Brooks laugh.

Princess climbed on the beam. Even though she was only eight years old, she took gymnastics seriously. She prided herself on becoming the next Simone Biles. If she could, she would sleep, eat, and breathe gymnastics. Oh, and let's not forget, her father. She loved them both the same.

Princess did her normal routine. For an eight-year-old, she really knew what she was doing. "Good, Princess! Good!" Coach Brooks complimented her. "Now, three-sixty." Princess nodded and did a quick three-sixty on her tip toes. "Good, darling, again!" Coach Brooks instructed.

Princess followed her instructions. From where I was sitting, Princess looked tired. Like she was out of breath. But she did as her coach instructed. As Princess did another three-sixty, she collapsed over the side of the beam, landing on a mat.

"Oh God!" I ran from my seat to my daughter. By the time I got to the other side, Coach Brooks was already there. Princess' head was resting on her leg. Her legs looked as if they were barely moving. Her eyes were glossy.

"Baby, are you okay?" Princess did not respond to me; she just stared.

I snatched my iPhone from my bra and dialed 9-1-1.

***

Memphis

I finished my so-called shift of passing out juice and water. I was a little tired, but I wasn't going to bed. I still had to work my shift on the wing, cleaning and mopping once everyone racked up.

I had made a few sales when I was in the hall. A quick fifteen hunnit. A nice day's work. I was going to let baby rest for the night then call her Asian ass tomorrow morning, bright and early. I figured Jessica and Princess were probably just now getting home from gymnastics.

"What's good, black man?" I greeted the African C.O. that was working the wing.

"Nothing much, yellow man," he responded. I could never pronounce his name, so I always greeted him by calling him black man. The first time I ever called him that, he replied by calling me, *yellow man*. Ever since then, that's how we greeted each other.

"Black man, are you tired?" I asked.

"Me no. I was in the United States Navy. This is easy work."

"You damn right." I laughed as I ran to my cell to change into my work clothes. My celly—Kingpen—was sitting at the desk, typing. He had his headphones on when I walked up to the cell. My door didn't pop, so I had to get his attention so he could grab a few items for me.

I waved my hands inside the bars to get his attention. He looked my way and took his headphones off. "You coming in?" he asked, willing to give me some alone time in the cell.

I shook my head. "Nawl, I'm 'bout to get ready fo' work. I need you to grab a few things for me." He stood up and walked to the bars.

"What do you need?" he asked.

"I need my coffee, cappuccino, like fo', or five mint sticks, then fireballs on the bottom shelf. Two Sprites, a box of them granola bars, uh-them Wheat Thins and like fo' pack of oatmeal. Just put it all in a commissary bag."

"Damn, what you 'bout to do, have a coffee and protein party?" he joked.

I laughed and said, "Nawl, I'm just getting everything I need for the night; that way I ain't got to bother up no mo'."

Kingpen gathered all of my items and tossed them inside my white commissary bag. "You ain't bothering me, bruh. If you need som', pull up."

"It ain't that. I know you not trippin'. I just be seeing you in yo' zone. I'on be wanting to fuck up yo' concentration."

"When I'm in my zone, can't nothing knock me out of it. What I got is a God-given talent. What comes to my mind could never be lost, feel me?"

I nodded. "I overstand! Get back to work though, I'm tryna buy yo' next novel."

He laughed at me. "Naw, you playing games."

I walked down the stairs. They had changed shifts. We had a cool African chick working. Majority of the shift was African. A lot of inmates didn't get along with the Africans. I did. I treated them how I wanted to be treated. With respect. And they gave it to me. It was Africans like BoBo, Johnson, Chike, BamBam, and Ms. Ezegi that made me respect the rest of Africans. Those few had paved the way for all Africans to come.

"Ms. Makali," I spoke. Ms. Makali was cool, but often misunderstood. She rocked three different wigs. One day she'll have on red hair, the next—black, and today, blonde. She was cool though. Lazy, but cool. She had a fat ass, and she often rocked these super tight, dark blue pants that made her ass more conspicuous. I had a lot of respect for her. I would always catch her doing her Bible study homework, or she would be talking to this African C.O. that I called, Preacher Man. Preacher was a real preacher; he just worked for TDC. Once I saw Ms. Makali talking to the preacher, she won me over.

"Where's your brother?" She asked for my other two co-workers.

I had two co-workers. My old-school young patna, Ninety-Nine. Ninety-Nine got his name for the exact amount of years he had, ninety-nine. He was a gangsta to the core. He was from Tyler, Texas but he went all the way to California to get put down with the crips. His little brother was an ex-NFL player who played cornerback, and kickoff returner for the Buffalo Bills. Ninety-Nine was my guy. We would stay up all night working out and talking about the real world. His little brother blessed him with a Maserati Ghibli as a present for when he made parole. Many nights we stayed up talking about riding around Texas in his Maserati, and his R.D.M. movement.

Our other co-worker had a punk name: MeMe. MeMe wasn't one of those lipstick eye shadow punks. He was a Hispanic from Austin, the O-2 section. He was cool, never the one to push up on you. He stayed out the way and did his job. Whenever new chicks would come around, he would always try to push them my way; it was odd, because a lot of female C.O.'s fucked with him and trusted his advice, kinda like he was their confidant or som'. But each shift would only allow two porters to work at a time, so mainly I would pay MeMe twenty, to fifty dollars a week to stay in the cell, depending on who's working.

Tonight, it was me, Ninety-Nine, and fine ass Ms. Makali. Or so I thought.

"Hey, mama." Ms. Davenport strutted to the gateway looking damn good. I looked at her wondering what she was doing here, because this wasn't her shift. I had just seen her on L-Wing.

"Hey, are you doing overtime?" Ms. Makali asked her.

"Um-huh. I'm on the keys right here, and they got me working the picket. So, you better make sure your count is right because I don't feel like doing no re-counts all night." Ms. Davenport looked at me. She had this sexy, seductive, mischievous look on her face. Like she was up to something.

Ninety-Nine walked up to me. "Well, I see you are about to be real busy tonight." He pointed at Davenport with his chin.

"Nawl, she's working the keys," I said, trying to pretend I didn't understand what he meant.

"Nigga, I've been gone twenty plus. I know when a nigga like a bitch, and I know when a bitch likes a nigga. Just be careful. Makali ain't no fool." He gave his advice and walked off.

"Rack time! Rack time!" Ms. Makali shouted across the dayroom. She was all smiles, knowing in the next thirty minutes she could be left alone. And to be honest, I was happy for her.

I walked up to the main gate as Makali started racking up the wing. "How'd you pull this off?" I asked Davenport.

She eyed me up and down, then she looked at her own shoes. She didn't have on the Skechers, but a pair of work boots.

"Oh snap, you upgraded," I teased.

She sucked her teeth. "Boy, be quiet." She smiled and said: "See, we ain't fin' to do this all night. I could've asked to work someplace else."

"Oh, you asked to work right here?" She blushed. "For who?" I asked.

She looked at me and licked her lips. "I got som' airheads, you want some?"

Chapter Twenty-One

Anastasia

I couldn't believe they actually let me work down here. When I asked the shift Lt. to let me do my OT on E, F, G, H block, I thought for sure he would turn me down, but he didn't. They were so short of staff; he was just happy that I'd stayed. I didn't expect Memphis to be the third shift porter, but I was glad that he was. That gives me eight hours to talk to him, and look at him, 'cause I swear he does something to my pussy.

As I let Ms. Makali off the wing to do her cross-count, Memphis stared at me. Without trying, I blushed. He made me feel like I was back in high school. I walked over to the cooler that I stole and used as a seat. I sat down and pulled my walkie-talkie off my hip to call the count in. I looked over to H-Wing, feeling that someone was watching. And he was.

I smiled and said, "Look the other way until I call my count in." He made me nervous in a good way.

"Why?" he asked.

I walked to the gates where he stood and said, "Because you make me nervous. I want to be able to concentrate." He smiled and sat down on a cooler inside the wing.

"Well, hurry up, I want to holla at you 'bout som'." I nodded and blushed. I walked off and called the count in.

Once I called my count in, I sat on the cooler and pulled out a pack of ranch style Doritos from my bag. "Boss Lady!" Memphis yelled.

"I'm tired," I said as I walked over to him with the chips in my hand. "What's up?"

"You know those are my favorite chips, right?" He looked at me and smiled. I had to turn my head to keep from blushing.

"Really, well, you not getting any." I teased him by pulling out a chip, opening my mouth wide. I let him see me place the chip on my tongue. I closed my mouth and gasped.

"What's your name?" he asked.

"Ms. Davenport"

"I can read. I'm talkin' 'bout your first name."

"Boy, I'm not about to give you my first name."

"Since you're being cautious, I guess I'll start," he said. "My name is Joshua Curry. I'm from Memphis, as you already know. I just got here a month ago from the feds. I have a little girl whose name is Princess—" He kept going until I stopped him.

"Her name is Princess?" I asked.

"Yea," he smiled.

"My dad used to call me Princess. My real name is Anastasia. Why'd you name her Princess?"

"Because that's what she'll always be to me, no matter how old she gets. She'll always be my Princess."

His words made me blush. "That's so sweet. How old is she?"

"Eight, she's my whole world."

"I can tell. Your eyes light up when you say her name." I wished his eyes would do the same when he says my name.

"So, why'd you ask to work down here?" he asked. I was hoping he didn't bring the subject up. I really didn't know how to answer him without exposing my true feelings.

Spit it out, A-D. It's now, or never, I thought to myself. I folded my chips and sighed. "Okay," I said. "I've been having these dreams about you," I finally said.

He looked at me. No smiling, no smirks, and asked: "What were they about?"

"Us, you know. Doing—uh—grown folks stuff."

He laughed then got serious. "How did I perform?" Before I could say anything, he asked: "Where were we at?"

I blushed and pointed upstairs. "In the three-o-one closet." He nodded and bit his bottom lip. He made me want to make my dream a reality.

"That's what's up." He looked at my lips.

That's what's up, really? That's all he had to say, I thought.

"Tell me something about you," he said. I wanted to tell him everything, but one, I didn't know him, and two, I didn't think he'll still like me if I did. That's if he even liked me.

"Nah, I can't," I said.

"Why not?"

"Because you're not ready for the real A-D."

"Try me."

I sighed. Before I could start, he said: "I don't ever want to see you crying in front of these ma'fuckas ever again." The way he said it made my pussy jump. I nodded like he was my daddy.

I started telling him about my life. How old I was. That I had graduated high school and started going to college. I told him about my dreams of working in the Air Force. I told him about my family. The bond me and my mom had.

Then he asked, "Why are you working here if you're in college?"

"I dropped out," I shyly said. "I would always fall asleep in class, so I just gave up."

"Why were you always asleep?"

"Because I would party hard the night before." He nodded as I continued my life story. I told him how my sister put the idea in my head to come work here. She said I would like it, and she was right.

"What kind of men are you into?" he asked.

I stared at him, hoping he could see his own reflection in my eyes because he was my type. "Uhm, it depends."

"Oh?" he countered.

I blushed. "I like thugs, but smart ones. Niggas that got their shit in order. He has goals. To me, he doesn't have to have a lot of money, because I'm not materialistic. I'm the type that will settle for hugs and kisses, instead of diamonds and pearls."

"Your last boyfriend, what was he like?" I was hoping his topic of questions would switch up so I wouldn't have to relive my past, 'cause I wasn't proud of it.

"I haven't had a boyfriend in a while," I said.

"Why not?" *He was not going to quit, ugh*! I thought to myself.

"Because I—I have a past."

"Don't we all?" he said, then added: "Let it out."

"If I tell you, I'm afraid you'll judge me for it."

"I'm not God, ma. That's his job."

I sighed. "When I was in high school, I got drunk and high at a party. These two dudes that I knew from school invited me back to their hotel room. We got high again." I exhaled, wondering if I should continue.

You've come this far, I thought to myself.

I continued. "I ended up letting them both run a train on me *on camera.*"

There, I did it! I thought to myself. I looked at him, embarrassed as I wondered what went through his mind. He didn't say anything for almost a full minute. I felt like I lost him before he even became mine.

"Did they drug you?" he asked.

I shook my head. "No. I knew what was going on." His eyes shut close. Almost immediately, his eyes opened. I knew he probably thought I was a slut, thot, freak, all of the above. But that was in high school. I am grown now. I mean yes, I still had some freak in me, but my train days were over.

"I knew I shouldn't have told you." I said, on the verge of tears.

"You did the right thing," he said. "The only way I can show you your past doesn't matter is that we have to start from scratch. That's the only way we can build. That means, pulling up every piece of wood and carpet in the closet. See, a lot of people want to build, but they don't want to empty their skeletons out the closet first. I like yo' style. In fact, I liked you from the first moment I laid eyes on you. It takes a strong woman to expose what you just exposed. I salute you for that. But—"

Oh fuck, I thought. *Here it goes.*

"Once you clean out your closet, and we start remodeling on a more solid foundation, the price of the house will go up. But, the price will go back down as soon as you start filling it back up with skeletons. I'ma tell you right now, me, I'm free-world. This is not my final resting place. I don't have fifty, or a seventy-year sentence. I'll be home soon. So, what are you gonna do?"

"What do you mean?" I was confused.

"I want you to fuck with me. But, it has to be your choice. I gave you just enough time to see every nigga on the unit. By now, you should've picked you at least one."

"Who says I'm looking?"

"Your heart! I heard it as soon as you walked on the unit. Now, I'ma ask you again. What you gon' do? 'Cause once the train leaves, it doesn't come back."

Damn, this black ass nigga too smooth! I thought to myself.

I looked around. It was count time again. "Memphis, give me some time and I'll let you know."

He looked at his wrist. "It's a reason I don't wear watches, 'cause I'on got time." He stood up and walked away.

My walkie-talkie went off. It was scout time. I wanted to scream his name and call him back, but I couldn't. I was still a C.O., and I had a job to do.

Chapter Twenty-Two

The Next Day

Hotboy

Me and my co-worker Ronnie rode around in the TDJC issued garbage truck. Today I would finally be able to go to the Beto Unit. Eastwood had informed me that he started back working in the sign shop, and that he was waiting for me to show my face.

The plan was simple. Once I got inside the gate, the guards would search the truck, then let us pass. All of the phones and drugs would be under the dump, under a lot of trash. I already have everything separated. Eastwood was to have his own workers. Inmates would pick up the drop and sneak it back inside the building. The plan was simple and could be successful if it were done right. Being that we only came once a week to empty the trash, the drops would be big. Thirty phones, and thirty cans of tobacco.

"Are you ready?" Ronnie asked me as we pulled up to the back gate to get on the unit. Ronnie knew the whole play. I had paid him five grand to go along with the plan.

Pulling up to the Beto Unit gave me chills. The last time I was here, I went through hell. Even though I wasn't in white anymore, if someone was to recognize my face, I would be back in white, or worse—Dead.

"Just be cool, nigga. Show your ID and stay calm," Ronnie said, obviously seeing the nervousness written on my face. Ronnie pulled inside the gate; it closed behind us. We were locked inside a cage large enough to fit an eighteen wheeler. A Caucasian male C.O. walked around the truck with a mirror on a long stick as he looked under the truck through the mirror. After we passed the test, we were asked to show ID's. I recognized the C.O. He'd just started working the unit when I was planning my escape. The inmates had given him the nickname, *Superman* because he wore glasses that made him look like Clark Kent.

Superman looked at Ronnie's ID then his face. He handed his ID back. I passed mine to Ronnie so that I wouldn't have to reach over him. I had Lakewood's ID. His picture was dark, so his face was barely visible. I wore a TDC-issued hat, so the top of my face was barely visible. Superman looked at my ID then to me, then back to Ronnie, then he waved us through.

I sighed in relief. We made it!

Ronnie drove to the back dock behind the unit. He parked and we both jumped out. "Let's make it quick," he said as he jumped back in the driver's seat. He lined the front of the truck with a dumpster and started the process of picking it up.

Meanwhile, I was behind the trash truck unloading corn cans that are full of phones and tobacco. I stacked the cans up behind a greaser and walked around to the front of the truck. Ronnie looked at me. I nodded, letting him know the job was done. I climbed back in the truck and closed the door. I was a little disappointed that I didn't get to see Eastwood, but maybe it was for the better. Who knows who else would have recognized me.

After Ronnie finished emptying all of the dumpsters, we passed through the same way we came in.

***

Eastwood

"Stay in your pairs!" Mr. Terry the sign shop C.O. yelled as we headed back in the building after a hard day of free labor. "Now I want y'all to stay with your pairs. The wardens are here, and they're walking around. Stay fully dressed until I call your names."

I looked around for my mules. I had met this tall white boy named Stretch who introduced me to some of his white friends. I guaranteed them all a phone, and one can of tobacco apiece to sneak everything back inside. Lord knows I wasn't going to do it.

Like clockwork, I noticed five inmates dressed in white jumpers and white hats started to clean up the excess trash. Simultaneously, they would tuck something inside their jumper from inside a large can. I smiled and nodded. Now all they had to do was make it back inside.

***

Memphis

"Get up, bitch!" I flinched as someone touched my feet. I hated when people touched my feet. I pulled the sheet from off my face and looked through tired eyes.

"What do you want, Stretch, bitch!" I yelled as I sat up in my bunk.

Stretch was a tall Caucasian inmate. He was pushing six foot eight inches. He had a bald head with a big bushy, dirty blond beard. He rocked prison-made gauges in his ears, and a pair of Armani Exchange glasses over his eyes. He stood in front of my cell with a wife beater on a pair of white shoes, and a pair of bloody red socks, with his white Reeboks.

Stretch had slid back from his racist brotherhood and went solo. But being that he hung around the homie Mack, he started talking black, and he started rocking red socks like he was one of the homies.

"Get up, bitch, you can't sleep all day!" Stretch said as he leaned his back against the rail outside my cell.

I scratched my head through my du-rag. "My nigga, I really just went to sleep." I looked at my clock. It was time for the sign shop to come back. I usually would sleep the entire first shift and get up once the second shift came.

"We got som' major shit going today. I need you to hold Jigga." I shook my head at him. "Fo'real, my nigga'," he added.

I looked at him with an expression to kill. Stretch said the word nigga like he invented it. I stood up and stretched. I was still a little sleepy, but what the hell! I figured I might as well get up. My celly was about to come back anyway.

"Is he asleep?" I heard a familiar voice ask Stretch. Stretch nodded as Lil Ru walked up to my cell. Lil Ru was a crip from

137

Dallas. He was about five foot three. He had a little man complex, but he was quick to fight. He wore a fro-hawk, and he had a diamond grill in his mouth.

"What's up, bitch? Come out and fuck with me," Lil Ru said.

"Who's working?" I asked as I started brushing my teeth.

"Ms. Wild, the new white girl, but she 'bout to go in a minute. Lil' bitch ain't no police like I thought she was. But the sergeant kept pulling up on the wing for her."

"You know what that means?" I said.

"Yea, either he's tryna fuck, or he already did," Lil Ru said.

"Fasho! Get my door open. I'ma come out," I said as I started getting dressed.

As Lil Ru walked off, Stretch stepped closer to my cell. "Fire me up, bitch," he said, wanting to smoke a cigarette; he did that shit every morning. He'll wake me up, make small talk, then ask me to smoke one with him. Weak ass game!

"My nigga, you know you got all my squares. Why you just didn't roll one up?" I had moved all of my dope, tobacco, and phones to his spot because all he talked about was how the laws never checked there, and that he made it through four lockdowns in the same spot. So, I trusted him, 'cause I gave him the benefit of the doubt, hoping I wouldn't regret it later.

My cell door rolled. I waked out and closed the door back. I walked to Stretch's cell on three row. He stayed in three-o-two. His door was automatic. I shook the door open, then sat on his bunk.

"Grab the smoke, and get one of those jags out, too!" I said to Stretch.

"Which one?" he asked.

"The flip." I had to call babymama to see how she was doing. I know she was probably pissed that I didn't call the night before.

Stretch came back in the cell and tossed the flip phone on my lap. He sat at his desk and rolled up a cigarette the size of his pinky. He lit a wick and lit the tip of the cigarette up. Tossing the wic in the toilet, he kicked back and enjoyed the harsh tobacco.

I dialed Jessica's number. She answered on the first ring. I plugged Stretch's headphones in. "Can you hear me?" I asked her.

"Why didn't you call or answer any of my text?" She sounded as if she had been crying.

"Because we had a bad shift last night," I lied. "Plus, the message don't come through until I turn the phone on."

"It's Princess," she said.

"What about her?" I asked.

"She's in the hospital. She caught Corona."

I shook my head, not believing her. I had thought kids couldn't catch Corona. "How? She's only eight. I thought kids couldn't catch it!"

"The doctor said her immune system was weak. You know she has asthma, but that's not all." It sounded like she had started back crying

I rubbed my waves backwards, not believing what she was saying. "What else?" I really was afraid to ask.

"The doctor said she's not looking good. That she has a weak heart. He doesn't think her heart is strong enough to recover from it."

I shook my head as the tears started to fall. How could a loving, innocent eight-year-old whose heart had love for the entire world not be strong enough!

"Can I talk to her?" I wanted to hear my little girl's voice.

"She's asleep. She just came from getting a CAT scan. Do you really want me to wake her?"

"Fuckin' right! Let me talk to my daughter!" I spat. I didn't mean to snap at Jessica, but my anger got the best of me. Princess was the love of my life. My seed. My better half. She was the only good I ever did in this cold cruel world.

"He-ll-o," her voice cracked into the phone. I had to cover my mouth with my hand so she wouldn't hear me crying. I wanted her to think her daddy was strong.

After I got myself together, I said: "Hey, Princess, how you doing?"

"I-I'm sick, daddy. I don't, fe-el good," she said in a whisper.

The tears started raining down my face. "It's going to be okay, baby girl. I promise. Daddy's going to make sure you get well, I promise."

"I-I know you will, daddy. C-can I come and visit soon?"

I nodded as if she could see me. "Yeah, Princess, you, me and mommy. As soon as you get better, mommy will bring you. We can eat all the skittles you want."

"Okay, daddy."

Jessica came back on the phone. "Josh, I'm losing it. I don't know what to do anymore," she cried.

"How does she look?" I asked.

"She looks tired. The nurses and doctors keep injecting her with so many different medicines." She sighed and said: "I wish you were here. She asked about you all day."

"Since I'm not, you have to be strong for her. Don't let her see you cry. We're going to get through this, I promise. She'll get through this. She's a Curry. She's strong!"

"Okay, uhm, the nurses are telling me I can't use my cell phone in the hospital, so I'll text you the number to her room. I love you."

"I love you too!" She blew me a kiss and I hung up. I snatched the headphones off and let my emotions show. I cried for close to a minute with my face in my hand.

Stretch patted my leg. I looked up to see a freshly lit cigarette. I took it and inhaled it like the tobacco could erase my pain. It gave me a light head, but the pain was still there.

What's wrong?" Stretch asked.

I recapped everything to him exactly how Jessica explained it to me. Once I finished, Stretch was in tears. "Damn, homie, I'ma keep her in my prayers.

I nodded.

"I'ma give you a lil' alone time to clear yo' mind," he said as he dap'd me up.

I sat back on his bunk as I smoked the cigarette until I felt the *doobie* burn my finger. I had to find a way to release all the anger I had inside. And I knew just how to do it.

Chapter Twenty-Three

Eastwood

After I showered, I waited patiently for Stretch's homeboys to come through the back door with the drop. It took them thirty minutes, but they finally showed up. They didn't know the play was for me, so I pretended like I didn't know what was going on. My purpose of staying and waiting was to make sure they didn't try to pull a fast one. If they did, part two of my killing spree was gon' be on their ass.

They talked amongst themselves as they tossed everything in four different commissary bags. They concealed everything with clothes. I walked out the shower behind them, trailing them to the wing. As we were let on the wing, they ran up the stairs to Stretch's cell. I stopped and looked for the wing boss. "You just came in from the sign shop?" C.O. Wild asked.

I nodded as I looked at her. Ms. Wild was a sexy Caucasian white girl with wide hips, and a teardrop booty. She had blonde hair with dirty blonde streaks. She had a pretty face, but a ball shaped head. I looked at her neck; she had passion marks on both sides that were black and purple.

"Got damn, ma! You got to stay away from them vampires," I laughed.

She played it off cool, calm and collected. I burned myself with a curling iron," she lied.

I laughed. I liked her style. Innocent until proven guilty.

"That's none of my business. I was just shooting the shit. But, I will say this. That—" I pointed, "is one or two things. Either you got som' bomb ass pussy, or an insecure nigga. Like I said, it could be one or the other, or both." I walked off, leaving her to decide.

I passed by Stretch's mules as I walked to his cell. Stretch had a lot of niggas in front of his cell like it was a block party. I looked at him, like, *what the fuck*!

"I'ma holla at y'all later," Stretch said to Mack and a few other people.

I walked in his cell. Behind the sheet that he had hung up, there were six big bundles sitting on his desk all wrapped in black tape.

"Did you pay them yet?" I asked.

He shook his head. "Nawl, I was waiting on you. I told them I would pull up at last chow."

"Bet, start bustin' that shit open." I grabbed a razor and helped him. It took us twenty minutes to unwrap everything. Once we finished, we were staring at thirty ZTE touch screen phones, fifteen universal chargers, thirty-eight ounce cans of rolling tobacco, and ten SIM cards.

"Damn, this a lot of shit. Where are we gon' stash all this shit at?" he asked.

"That's yo' job. You keep a jag, and a can. Pay the mules and put the rest up." I walked out his cell, leaving him dumbfounded.

"Lil Ru!" I called after him.

"What's up?"

I leaned to his level and whispered. "Spread the word that you got jags for sale, fifteen hunnit apiece. The first ten come with a charger. Cans of tobacco goin' for fo' hunniit."

Lil Ru's eyes lit up. "Overstood, I gotcha! I'ma spread the word right away.

"Aye, Stretch!" I yelled upstairs. Stretch walked to the stair rail. "Where is Memphis at?'

Stretch shrugged. "I think he left to take care of some business."

***

Memphis

I snatched a jumper from the laundry, and a pair of yard gloves from the chemical closet. I had the shank that I'd taken from McFee's office tucked under my waistband. I strolled down the hallway like I didn't have a care in the world. I had one agenda on my mind: find Turk.

With the news from my daughter, I had to clear my head. And the only way I could do that was to make sure someone felt my pain. I felt that there was no one better to hurt than the nigga who had wronged my daughter.

As I was walking to the northside, a couple of people saluted me and asked for my cash app to buy some dope. I told them to hold off on sending any money until later. I had other business to tend to at the moment. I bumped into an inmate that was coming from the northside commissary window.

"My bad, homie," I said as he was about to close the north commissary hall door. I caught a glimpse inside the short hallway and noticed my victim was arguing with the commissary lady.

"What the fuck you mean y'all goin' on break! I'm the last person!" Turk yelled at the commissary lady. I slid in the small, barely lit hallway and acted like I was going to use the toilet.

"See, y'all on som' bullshit, y'all know y'all can run my ID and get me out of the way!"

"Sir, we'll only be gone thirty minutes for lunch; we'll come back," the lady tried to reason.

"Fuck you, lazy ass bitch you can—" the lady slammed the small double doors in his face. Turk punched the metal doors like he was Superman. "Bitch!" he spat as he picked up his commissary bags from off the floor.

As he was about to walk out the hall, I snatched him back by the collar of his shirt and punched him as hard as I could in his eye with a right hook. I closed the door as Turk stumbled backwards.

I stepped under the light so that he could see my face. Once he recognized me he said, "Oh, I've been waiting on this." He rubbed his watered eye and balled up his fist.

I threw a double jab. He dipped my punches and scooped me up, slamming me on the ground. The impact made me a little dizzy as I bumped my head on the ground. Turk started raining blows on my head and body as I covered up to block the blows.

"Bitch ass nigga, you tried to sneak me!" he said as he tried to punch through my guard.

I raised my knee and kneaded him in his balls. He fell over and I jumped to my feet. I kicked him in his face. He rolled over in pain, damn near kissing the toilet.

"Get up, bitch nigga!" I squared up. Turk stood up, still holding his balls. He squared up with me. I faked a jab, making him slip. I countered him with a right hook right to his head. I felt his skull crack my knuckle. I was glad I wore gloves, because I knew my knuckles were probably bleeding.

Turk stumbled and hit the brick wall. I threw a mean combination of hooks and uppercuts as he fought to keep his balance. My last punch sent him reeling into the toilet. I unbuttoned my jumper and stuck my hand in my boxers. Turk saw me and weakly shook his head.

"Come on, folk," he said, thinking I was about to rape him. I pulled out my shank. His eyes lit up. He jumped up to run. I clipped him with my leg, sending him sliding across the floor. As he crawled, I walked towards him. I pulled him by his leg, then kicked him.

"You touched my daughter!" I kicked him again.

"Folk, it wasn't even like that," he pleaded as I kicked him again.

"You shouldn't have laid a finger on her. Fuck yo' pleas, and yo' intentions!" I slid the shank into his stomach. It came back out like a butter knife.

"Ahh! Help!" he screamed as I kicked him hard in the face again. His head hit the wall, knocking him unconscious. My mind drifted to my little girl laying in a hospital bed fighting for her young life. I envisioned her looking sick and helpless. Her mother is sitting at her bedside praying to God. I started crying as I raised the shank above my head like Michael Myers. I came down hard, stabbing Turk repeatedly in his chest and neck. His body jerked as blood spurted from his mouth. I blacked out as I stabbed him thirty or more times. Once I came to, there was blood everywhere

My body started shaking. My nerves were shot. I pulled his body to the back of the hall. The visitation gate was open. I slid his body in the cage and closed it. In a rush, I washed off all the blood

I could off my face, arms, and hands. I then stripped out of the jumper, thankful that I'd thought to wear another regular set of clothes under it. I balled the jumper up and looked around the floor for anything that could connect me to the scene. Seeing nothing, I wiped the sweat from my face and walked out the hall, closing the door behind myself.

Once in the main hall, I took the gloves off and blended in with the traffic of inmates going up and down the hallway. I noticed Big Tank as he was pushing the juice cart up the hall. "I was with you all day, okay?" I said to Big Tank. He looked at me and nodded, no questions asked.

As we were walking down the hall to the far north end, we stopped in front of P-wing, which was medium custody, G4 status. They had a big fire going in front of the gate because they didn't like the food they were fed in their Johnnies. I tossed the bloodied jumper and gloves in the fire. The flame caught on to the clothes and gloves.

"Thank you, homie!" an inmate on P-Wing said, thinking that I had added to the fire to help their cause.

"Nawl, thank you!"

Chapter Twenty-Four

Lt. McFee

I walked on the unit after being away on paid leave for two weeks. The unit major called my phone and informed me that someone had been murdered, stabbed to death in the north commissary hallway. When I saw the news, my mind went straight to Gianni Kingsley. But he was dead now.

"Did anyone see anything?" I asked sergeant Lander as I looked at the crime scene

Sergeant Lander shook his head. "Nope. I talked to the commissary lady and she said, close to an hour ago, her and the deceased inmate had a verbal argument because she didn't run his ID for commissary. She said she slammed the window and left. After their lunch break, she came back and called for a host of commissary. As the inmates came down to make store, they noticed all of the blood and reported it. When I was down here, I followed the blood leading to the visitation hall, that's how I found the body."

I nodded as I looked at the dead inmate. He looked as if he had a fight with Edward Scissorhands. By estimate, he looked to have been stabbed over twenty times.

"Okay, good work, Lander. Let's close this hall off until the police get here. Rack the unit up, you can leave out the hallway porters." Sergeant Lander nodded and walked away.

I went to my office and looked in my desk drawer. I pulled out my secret weapon, which was pictures of inmates that I got from cell phones that I confiscated. I saved the pictures for when I needed information. I scanned through the pictures until I landed on the right one.

Bingo!

***

"Fatty Mack, have a seat," I said to the brown-skinned inmate. Fatty Mack was just another inmate who took pictures with camera phones, flushed the phone, and thought everything would be good, not knowing I had friends in high places.

Fatty Mack looked at me as he wondered how I knew his street name. "Why am I down here?" he asked.

"I need some information, and you're going to give it to me." I typed on my computer, pulling up his crime and mug shot.

"It says you're due to see parole in the next ten months."

"Yea, so!" he bluntly said.

I looked at the computer. "Fatty Mack, I want to know what's going on. Who's doing what on my unit, and you're going to tell me. I want to know who's fuckin' who, and who's dropping off."

"I'on know," he said. I pulled his photo shoot camera phone picture from my drawer and slapped it on my desk right in front of him.

"You do know I don't need to catch you with a phone to prove you had one. As long as I got this picture of you parlaying in the cell, I got you in Anderson County getting two-to-five more years stacked!"

Fatty Mack's face lit up. I could see his spit caught in his throat. His mouth opened, but I stopped him. "I hope your next words will be a statement that will get me to make this picture disappear. I tell you what, give me what I want, and I'll act like we never saw this. I'll have you on the next chain bus smokin' to another unit."

He thought about it for a second. "Fatty Mack, be smart. If you don't tell me, I'm still going to go back to your wing and lie like you did, then I'm going to place you back on the same wing and turn the cameras off. You only have nine fingers right now. By the time I see you again, you might only have one hand so?"

Fatty Mack knew I was capable of doing exactly what I said. Someone had left me a note that said, *Let the games begin*. They wanted to play, so I was about to play. But I played by my own set of rules.

"Okay," he said, "all I know is Baby G and Ms. Patricia messing around. I used to watch out for them while they fucked in the upstairs infirmary."

"What else?"

"Rumor is this nigga Memphis got the cheapest prices on Beto right now for everything. Phones, tobacco and K2."

"What's his real name?"

"I'on know. He stayed on H-Wing. I-I think his name is C-Curry or sum like that." He kept going until I had a list of dirty C.O.'s and inmates. It was just that easy. The reason I was so good at what I did had nothing to do with skill but everything to do with snitches. Without them, I had nothing. With them, I had multiple convictions!

Chapter Twenty-Five

Anastasia

I sat my lazy ass down in A-Wing's empty dayroom as I fixed the table up to my likings. I was finally out of the jungle and now I was working in the 'burbs. The Lt. blessed me by letting me work on the easiest wing on the unit, A-Wing. A-Wing had been transformed into an intake, so every inmate on the wing was new to the system. The only thing they were allowed to do was go to chow, and to the dayroom. Considering the warden locked the unit down, it was just me and my bag of snacks. I had the TV on, getting ready to watch the Grammys. Work or not, I was not gon' miss Megan Thee Stallion's performance.

I walked around, giving the inmates a fair look of my ass, and swished up and down the run. Majority of them were jacking off while their celly was either asleep or pretending. After I gave them a show, I went back to the dayroom. I was starting to get hungry. I bought me a subway sandwich, a big bag of Doritos, a bag of airheads, some Funyuns which were my favorite chips, and some Winterfresh to clean up the aftermath.

"Eliz!" I yelled for the keyboss. Eliz was a skinny, country cowgirl that I had befriended while I was on OJT. Eliz was cool, sometimes. I would talk to her about certain things but never about my personal life. For reasons that I felt was out of pressure, she would tell everything to me. There's no such thing as too much pressure, just weak pipes.

Eliz walked up to the gate. "Hey, boo!" She always greeted me like that, like she wanted to be my girlfriend-girlfriend. I sensed a little Bi-curious in her.

"Are they going to call chow or what?" I looked at the time on my little pink Walmart watch.

"No, they're bringing Johnny sacks in a minute."

"Who's gon' pass 'em out. I sho'll ain't 'bout to take my lil' ass up no three rows of stairs and pass 'em out."

"I'll help!" I looked to the side of Eliz to my superman.

"Memphis, what are you doing out? You are not a hallway porter," Eliz said, policing. And that's why I never told her my business because when it came down to save face, she would definitely point the finger.

"Just chill," Memphis said.

"No, you're not about to get me in trouble," Eliz said.

"Let him help me, Eliz—" I poked my lips out. "Cos I ain't passing them out."

Eliz sighed and said: "Just make sure you get on count when they call it. She looked at him and opened the gate. He nodded and walked on the wing.

"Hol' 'em up." Big Tank ran on the wing. "Y'all can't forget about me."

Eliz laughed and shook her head as he locked the gate back. Big Tank walked in the dayroom and started going through my sack of goodies. "Oh-hh, we-ww! Memphis, look!"

Memphis walked in the dayroom and stood beside him. "She was 'bout to throw down without us," Big Tank said as he dug from him.

"You can't bring my favorite chips and expect not to share again," Memphis said.

"It depends on how hard you work," I smiled. "Then maybe I'll give you *some*." He looked down at my pussy print and licked his lips.

"Y'all so nasty," Big Tank said as he walked to the TV. "Yea, Memph', do the cleaning and whatnot. I'm just gonna sit right here and wait on Card—what's her name?"

"Cardi B," Memphis said.

"Yea, Cardi B, and that horse Stallion to perform." He had me and Memphis laughing hard. As I stopped laughing, Memphis stared me.

"What?" I asked, avoiding his piercing stare.

"You ready or what?"

I blushed. "And if I'm not, the train will leave, right?"

He nodded. "So?"

"I'on know, Memphis." I huffed. "I like you, I do. But I know you're going to expect something from me, and I'ma tell you now, I'm not bringing you anything in this prison."

"I don't want you so you can bring me something," he said.

"So, why do you want me?" I was really curious.

"First, 'cause of yo' lips. I've been dying to kiss them." I blushed. "Secondly, I wanted you from the first moment I laid eyes on you. I can't lie, I'ma playa. I fuck a lot of hoes, ask about me. But, I'll change my game for you. If you say yea', the pimp in me will die and wither away." He stopped then continued. "Accept me as I am, like I'm accepting you. Let's build on a new foundation. Something solid, unbreakable. I guarantee you won't regret it."

"If I say yes—" I said.

"When you say yes, I'ma pull you close to my heart and drown you in my love. I'll do whatever it takes to make your heart beat better."

I blushed at his smooth words. I felt that his words were a game, but it was a game I'd yet to play, and I was curious of what the outcome would be.

I huffed and said, "Okay. I'll give us a try. But just know, Memphis, if you break my heart, I'll never be the same. This is a first for me. Somehow, I feel that you put a spell on me, but I'm glad you did."

He smiled and nodded. "You won't regret it."

***

Memphis

I felt good with myself. I'd accomplished two goals in one day. First, I handled that fool—Turk. Then I made myself out to not be a liar by bagging the baddest bitch in the whole unit. Don't get me wrong, I liked her, she was cool. Her personality was on a thousand. She had a body out of this world, and she kept herself up. She was everything a street nigga would want. But I had yet to test her loyalty.

I know I sound like a hypocrite speaking on loyalty when I had a whole baby mama at home. What we were, was family. And what we had, was an understanding. As long as she didn't have a kid by another nigga, she was free to do her, and vice versa. Being that my little girl was in the hospital, I had to do something to keep my mind off of everything. So, I put my mind on the money, and thotties.

I told Anastasia about my daughter's situation. She teared up and said she would keep Princess in her prayers! I respected her and liked her more for that.

I finished passing out all of the Johnnies along with cold water. I was waiting for everyone to finish eating. I strolled over to Anastasia. I leaned my back against the wall away from the camera. I looked at her as she started blushing.

"Can't I taste those lips today?" I asked.

"Why you wanna kiss me so bad? You keep asking 'bout my lips."

"Cos I like 'em." I held my hand out to her. "Come here."

She held her hand out as she walked up to me. She drew it back. "The camera!"

"The camera can't see right here," I assured her. She smirked and said. "How do you know? You did this before?" I shook my head and said, "I just do my homework." I licked my lips. "Let me get some of them lips." She blushed again.

"I'm scared!"

"Gur', give that boy a kiss and stop lying. Hell, ain't nobody watching!" Big Tank yelled from the dayroom. We laughed at him. She sighed and walked off. She faced the wall opposite of me and shook her hands, I guess to shake the jitters. "One kiss, right?" she said. I wasn't sure if she was talking to me or herself. "I can do that." She faced me now.

She walked up to me, my back against the wall. "One kiss, right?" she said as she looked into her eyes. I nodded.

I stopped her and said. "Look, if you don't want to, you don't have to. I've never wanted you to do something that you don't feel comfortable doing. I'll like you regardless."

She nodded and stared into my eyes. She didn't know, but my eyes were the voodoo she was aligned about. I pulled her into me. For a brief second, I looked into her eyes. Then all I saw were fireworks as our lips touched. I don't know what got into her, but she took over. Our kiss felt like we were making love on the beach, with unlimited stamina.

As we pulled apart, she blushed and walked off a short distance. "Oh, my God!" she said to herself. "I really just did that!" She started to panic, then said. "You got me so wet right now."

I laughed. "Come here." I held my hand out to her.

"Uh-Uh, I can't! Not right now. I'on know how I'ma act."

I laughed again. "Come here, ma." She shook her head. "See, you're playing games."

She blushed. "I love when you say that."

"You are playing games," I said with my hand out to her. She walked into my embrace. I turned her so her back was against me. Her ass rested on my dick. I knew she could feel me poking at her ass. She felt good in my arms, like it was meant to be. She tried to walk away. I pulled her back; her juicy ass felt the bulge of my dick.

I don't know what happened. The way she kissed me; it fucked my head up. I had never been kissed like that, ever. I held her, neither of us saying anything. Neither of us caring where we were. As I held her, a song came to my mind.

Hold on, hold on, hold up daddy, what the fuck you doing/ You can annihilate way more chicks than the chick you screwin' / You on top of your game, homie, man you a star/ You got real bitches, they love that nigga that you are / They say you're like Jemi Hendrix in his early twenties / You a player, huh, you wanna come around and save her / You mad ill, I knew you'd be the one to keep it real / And I can't even lie dawg, when I see y'all it give me chills / And I'mma stand behind y'all because I know the way you live / Aye, just do me this favor, give it time, time reveals.

***

I spent damn near the whole night with Anastasia. Me, her, and Big Tank watched the Grammys together. Anastasia got jealous at how I was watching Megan Thee Stallion twerk. I laughed hard at that. She ended up sharing the food with Tank. I ate the chips and candy. Before I left for the night, we had our first argument, but we made up, and she gave me a fat, juicy, subway, breath kiss.

Me and Big Tank walked off the wing before the last count. As we were walking past D-Wing, I spotted Skittles leaning on the gate like something was bothering her. Before I could utter a word, Big Tank said, "Girl, you know my nephew Memphis like you. He talks about you all the time." Skittles smiled.

"Really?" She looked at me.

I looked at Big Tank. Not one time had I ever told him any such thing, but I could see what he was doing. I peeped the game a mile away. "Yea, I said.

"I can't tell. You didn't come by to say hi all day. You've been over there with Davenport all day."

I thought quickly. "That's because she didn't have any help, so I started watching the Grammys." I looked over her shoulder, one of my so-called homies named Rico was grilling me as he watched me interact with Skittles. I could see that he was salty behind it; I didn't care.

Like Young Dolph said, 'Don't play with me, play with yo' bitch!'

She smiled. "Look," I continued, "the only way I'ma fuck with'cha, is if you get under my wing. I've been hearing yo' name. I ain't second to nan', nigga. You feel me!" She nodded. "I'ma take you to the top." She smiled. "Are you ready to go to the top?"

"Yes," she replied.

"What's yo' number?" I only asked for it to see if she would give it to me. I had no intention of fuckin' with her. She already had a bad name for fucking a lot of African C.O.'s. I wasn't going in no pussy behind no African.

"214 777-5004," she said, shocking me. I nodded like I had a memory like an elephant and walked off.

Big Tank looked at me and said, "Boy, that Davenport gon' kill you, if she finds out about that white girl."

I looked at him stunned that he'd said that. "Nigga, you the one started it."

"Yea, but you finished it."

I laughed. "I did, didn't I?"

Chapter Twenty-Six

One Week Later

Hotboy

The money was rolling in faster than I could keep up. I made sure I separated my money from Eastwood's, then I would transfer my money to Steph's account. She was shocked to see how much money was being made. I was supposed to make another drop for Eastwood, but the unit was on lockdown for a murder. I was glad to hear Eastwood didn't have anything to do with it. I told him, the only way he can escape is out of lockup. But I knew once he started seeing all that money, trouble would be the last thing on his mind.

I sat at home on the porch beside Steph as we watched the twins play in the front yard. "If it's cool with you, I was gon' send Gabby some money." I looked at her to see her reaction. She sipped from her lemonade and said:

"I would expect you to." She never looked at me. "She is lonely, Gianni. I hate that for her."

"She has Jacob."

"Yes, she does. But she needs a male companion."

"She should try Craigslist," I joked, making her laugh. She sat her lemonade down. "She's still in love with you, you know that, don't you?"

"No, she's not."

"Oh yes, she is."

"How do you figure?" I was curious.

"She told me."

I looked at her. "Stop playing. She ain't flat out tell you no shit like that."

"No, not flat out. I asked her, and she denied it. I told her it's okay to still be in love with you, she came out and admitted it. She said she doesn't think she'll ever be able to love another man."

I sat and thought about what she said. "I hate that for her," I admitted.

"Me, too. That's the way I'ma give you a pass." She looked at me.

"A pass?"

"One pass. A pass to help her get you out of her system. I told her that we would be leaving Texas soon. I didn't tell her where, but I told her we would never return. So, I told her that I would let the two of you properly say your goodbyes."

I was shocked to hear her talk like that. She was always so protective of my dick. I laughed thinking this was some sort of set-up. I stood up and looked around.

"What are you looking for?" she asked.

"The cameras. I got to be getting punk'd!"

She laughed. "Sit down! Nobody is punking you. I'm being serious." She sighed. "I feel that you two need this. It's called closure. But with sex."

"Why are you doing this?"

"Because if the shoe was on the other foot, it'll break my heart to not be able to make love to you one last time before you ride off in the sunset with your new family." She stood up and kissed my lips. "Go make her day. I'll be here when you get back. I promise!"

I watched as Stephanie walked in the house. I was shocked, and horny as hell.

***

I used my spare key to Gabby's front door. I closed the door back as I called after her. "Gabby!"

"In the bedroom!" she yelled back. I shook my head and slowly walked towards her bedroom. I didn't know how I was going to even initiate sex with her to fulfill Stephanie's wish.

I walked to her bedroom door. The lights were dimmed. Candles were lit. Soft, sensual music by Chris Stapleton was playing, her lingerie thong set on. She walked up to me with a single red rose.

"Do you remember this song?" she asked, handing the rose to me. "It was the same song you first played when we had our first date in your cell." She stood on her tiptoes and kissed my lips.

'I've looked for love in all the same old places / Found the bottom of a bottle always dry / But when you poured out your heart I didn't waste it / 'Cause there's nothing like your love to get me high—'

Her kiss took me back to our very first kiss. How sweet her lips tasted then! I gripped her soft ass as our bodies traveled to her bed.

'You're a smooth as Tennessee Whiskey / You're as sweet as strawberry wine / You're as warm as a glass of Brandy / And honey, I stay stoned on your love all the time.'

"Gianni—" she moaned. I leaned up on my hands and looked in her eyes. "Please, just one last time, before I never see you again. Please, give me something to never forget you by. "Make love to me to where I'll be satisfied till my dying day. Put a stamp on my pussy so that if ever another man travels there, he'll know that it belongs to you."

Her words made my dick hard as hell. I nodded as I kissed her lips. I gave her everything she wanted, plus more.

'You're as smooth as Tennessee whiskey—'

Chapter Twenty-Seven

Lt. McFee

Slowly but surely, I've been going down my list of dirty C.O.'s that Fatty Mack had gave me. I ended up finding out who Memphis was; from the rumors I've been hearing, he has been selling anything he could get smuggled in. I placed him on my list, very close to the top.

"If you see these inmates in the hallway, strip them out, search all of their property and watch them very closely. Do not be fooled. They may seem innocent, they're not. They are slick and dirty. I have word that they are the cause of the recent drug flow." I passed around three different mugshots of offenders who were rumored to be moving drugs across the unit. One being Memphis.

I looked at C.O. Patricia. She didn't know, but for the past few days I've been tailing her, watching her movements as she traveled up and down the unit with her boo, Baby G.

"You all know what to do. Stay focused and alert!" I said, ending the shift briefing. I watched C.O. Patricia as she walked down the long O.D.R. hallway. I knew where she was headed. She didn't know that Fatty Mack had spilled the beans on which day she did her dirt.

As the room started spilling out, all of the C.O.'s went to their post. I gave Baby G and his crooked cop bitch just enough time to get settled in. I wasn't invited to join the fun, but I was about to crash the party.

***

"Ohmm!" Patricia moaned as he sucked Baby G's dick. I watched from a distance as she performed an oral cavity search on his dick. She was on her knees; he stood in front of her with his pants and boxers at his knees. He held his shirt up with his hands, making sure it didn't get in the way. Baby G kept rising to his tiptoes as the sensation took him to the edge.

She took her mouth from the head of his penis and jacked him off in circular motions with both hands. "You gon' fuck my pussy good?" she asked him, looking up from her knees.

"Hell, y-yeah!" he stuttered as he tried to hold his nut.

"Stand up!" he commanded. She stood, her little booty jiggling in her tight pants. She was a little taller than him, but he manhandled her like he was taller.

He snatched her, tilting her face to the wall. "Uhm, bae, you know I like it rough!" She flicked her tongue out, but he couldn't see it from behind her.

Baby G unbuttoned her pants and unzipped them. He snatched them down as he held her face close to the wall with his hand. To my amazement, he was bigger than I imagined. Her pink thong hid inside her ass crack. Baby G kneaded her legs apart. My own chest started to rise and fall as I watched them. I unzipped my pants, sucked my gut in, and felt around for my penis. I continued to watch them with my penis in my hand.

Baby G pulled the thong to the side and yanked it hard, tearing it completely off. He brought it to his nose and took a big whiff. "Do I smell ready?" she asked, face still planted to the wall.

"Let me see," he said, guiding his penis to her vagina. She squatted a little to help him, but once he pierced her opening, she stood straight up like a light. "Yea, you ready," he said as he fucked her, mushing her face to the wall. He fucked her fast and rough as he sandwiched her between the wall.

"Harder, babe!" she moaned. I didn't know when I'd started masturbating, but my hands were moving faster than I ever moved. Fifteen seconds later, I exploded.

"Urghh, ohhh, shit!" I nutted in spurts on the floor.

"What the fuck!" Baby G said as his dick made a popping noise as he pulled out of her vagina. I tried to hurry and get myself together before I was busted with my pants down. I was able to get my pants up, but the semen on the floor left me in a sticky situation.

"You're busted!" My chest heaved up and down as I tried to play it off while catching my breath. Before I could pick up my walkie talkie to call it in, Baby G punched me right in the face.

I started after him, but I slipped on my own semen. I ended up in a split, tearing myself a new asshole. Before I could recover, C.O. Patricia and Baby G jumped me. My walkie talkie fell to my side as Baby G kicked me in the face. After five more minutes of me getting my ass kicked, the blows stopped and I blacked out.

***

Memphis

My celly Kingpen was in the dayroom, so I finally had the cell to myself. Even though I needed some alone time, that wasn't the real reason I was in the cell. The real reason I was in the cell was because Skittles was working the wing, and Anastasia was working G-Wing. Which meant Anastasia had to come to my wing and cross-count. To prevent myself from getting caught up, I just stayed my black ass in the cell. Plus, Lil Ru had been chasing behind Skittles all day like she was his girl. I didn't care nonetheless; she was just something to do.

I was in the middle of writing Jessica a letter when Skittles walked up to my cell. "Why are you not out?" she asked with her hands on her hips.

"For one, my door is locked, and two, you already got yo' boyfriend out there with you."

"My boyfriend, who?" she countered.

"Stop playing that nigga ain't chasing yo' tail for no'n."

She laughed. "Who, Lil Ru?" She smirked and said, "He thinks something is going on, but it's nothing. I swear!" She leaned closer to the cell and whispered. "If you come out, I promise, I'll suck yo' dick off your body.

She had my full attention. I tossed Jessica's letter to the side and said, "Get the door open." She walked off, and five minutes later the door rolled.

I stepped out of the cell with my white shirt and shorts with my Cartier glasses on. I instantly noticed Lil Ru choppin' Skittles down.

I shrugged and walked to Lil D' cell. I walked inside and sat on his toilet.

"What's craken?" he asked.

"Mane, this lil' white hoe said she wanna suck my dick. I'on want bruh to get upset with me, 'cause I fuck with him, feel me? I'on know what I should do, 'cause I know he cuttin for the bitch.'

Lil D nodded. "The best thing you can do to avoid the bullshit, is to tell 'em.

"That what?"

"It all depends. 'Cause if he don't like her like that, y'all can run a train on the bitch. If he does like her, just fall back and see if he works clean. But, if she chooses you, it's fair game."

I nodded. "You right. Call 'em up here." Lil D walked out the cell, and a minute later, he came back with Lil Ru. My instincts told me that this shit was gon' go sideways, but I was thinking about it with my dick and not my brain.

I started off with. "You like this hoe?" Lil Ru looked at me, confused.

"Who?" he asked

"Skittles. Do you like her, like you tryna gal the hoe?"

He shook his head. "Nawl, why?"

I sighed, knowing better, but I still said it. "That hoe says she wanna suck my dick. I'm tryna make sure you ain't crushin' on her before I let her."

"I ain't tripping, she says she wanna suck my dick, too," Lil Ru said.

"That's live! Look, this how we gon' play it. Get the 3-0-1 closet open. I'ma tell her that its gon' be just me in there. I'ma go in. When she starts suckin' my dick, just come in with yo' shit out. But, if she says no, it means no. I ain't tryna get no rape case. Feel me?"

Lil Ru nodded. "I got'cha."

I walked down the stairs and told her of how I would be waiting in the closet, minus Lil Ru coming in. She nodded and agreed. I sat on the cooler as she did her rounds. I was supposed to wait until she made it to the back half of two rows so I could sneak up the stairs.

I noticed Lil Ru was in the closet. I shook my head. He was fucking the whole play up. I sat back and saw Skittles walk over three rows and made her way towards the closet. As she stopped in front of the closet, she screamed.

"What are you doing here?" She put her hands on her hips. "Get out of there, nasty!"

I shook my head and laughed. *Damn fool lied on his dick*, I thought to myself

Lil Ru ran downstairs in his feelings. "She only screamed 'cause them bitch ass nigga had their mirrors out the cell," Lil Ru said.

I laughed and thought, *let that be the reason.*

I walked up the stairs and dap'd my co-worker—Ninety-Nine—up. "What's a good, old timer?"

"Nothing much. I see you playing the game." He laughed. As we were conversing back and forth, Skittles walked past us and in a rushed tone, she said:

"Get him off my ass." As she walked by, so did Lil Ru. For a second, I thought I'd heard wrong, so I just kept talking to Ninety-Nine.

She came back in our direction; this time Lil Ru wasn't behind her. "Get him off my ass! We can't do anything with him following me around all night." She walked off.

I looked at Ninety-Nine, thankful that he had heard it with his own ears, and also thankful that he was a crip. Being that he was a crip, no one could say we were lying or hating on Lil Ru.

Ninety-Nine looked at me and said: "I'ma handle it." I nodded. I knew this was gon' be one hell of a night.

Chapter Twenty-Eight

Anastasia

I sat on the cooler by the gate. I didn't have anything against working G-Wing; I just wished I could be next door on H-Wing so that I can see my boo, Memphis. It sucked because it was like they knew we were an item, and having me work other wings was the way of keeping us apart. I had something for their ass though. I worked sixteen hour shifts a day. Eight hours on my shift, and eight hours OT just so that I could see him. Talk about loyalty. We would spend our nights together, as Memphis would say, building

I smiled as I thought about him. I swear, he gamed me up on niggas and the penitentiary. I can't lie, I hated how every woman on the unit worked H-Wing, but me. Today was no different. They had that Andy Milonakis looking ass bitch, who everyone called Skittles. She was the only reason I was seen sitting on the cooler looking like a stalker. The ugly ass bitch had a thing for my man. I knew 'cause one day me and her were sitting in the hallway together, then Memphis strolled by; she stopped him, saying: "Memphis, are you really from Tennessee?"

He laughed and said, "Yea, why?"

Boldly, the ugly ass bitch had the nerve to say: "I knew it, because you're the only ten-I-see."

She was lucky I didn't want to expose our relationship, because I was seconds from busting her upside her melon. When I asked Memphis about it, he denied they had anything going on. He made a lot of sense when he said, "You can't be mad at her for shooting her shot. She don't know we mess around, does she?" I shook my head. "Well, then she was just trying her luck. You should be happy that out of three thousand niggas on the unit, you get the flyest one."

His words made me cool down, but I still keep a close eye on that sneaky, hot pussy bitch like a hawk. I'd be damn if I let her slide in my spot.

My walkie talkie sounded like an indication that it was count time. I hated count time. Don't get me wrong, I never wrote any code twenties, which were masturbation cases. I didn't care that the inmates jacked off on me. But sometimes niggas took it to the extreme. Sticking their dicks out the bars, making me have to dodge their dicks like El Chapo dodged the FEDS.

As I walked down one row doing my count, the inmates were doing just what I expected: masturbating. I will admit, I looked at a few, blushed at some, but I kept it moving. I walked up the backstairs to two rows; the inmates were jacking off, too.

"Damn, when do y'all sleep!" I said to myself. I walked up to another cell to see how many inmates were inside. The inmate inside the cell shocked me.

The inmate wasn't masturbating. He was sitting on his bunk with not one, but two cell phones. He pretended not to see me as he counted out what looked to be close to five thousand dollars. I looked on in shock.

"Boy, what are you doing here?" I smiled. I knew who he was. His name was Sinbad. Everyone called him Sinbad because he looked like the character from the hit show, *Different World*. He had tried to get at me on Facebook one day. I turned him down and kept it to myself by not telling Memphis.

Sinbad thumbed through the big faces. "You want some?"

I shook my head. "How much is that?"

"A lil' chump change. Five racks. You want any?" He said it like he was caked up. Five grand wasn't a lot, but being that he had it in prison, it was a lot. But I still acted like it wasn't.

"I'm cool. That ain't no money. Don't impress me none." He laughed all cool like.

"Just let me know when you ready. I wish you'll come fuck with me and leave that nigga Memphis alone before he get you in trouble."

He shocked me when he said that. I wondered how he knew about me and Memphis. But then again, if you had eyes you could see. I literally worked OT on the same block, or I went home.

I simply said, "I'm cool. And who is Memphis? If I was messin' with whoever that is, you sho'll sound like you hatin' on him." I could hear him trying to explain himself as I walked off. I felt good that I didn't take the money. I couldn't wait to tell my baby; I know he will be proud of me. But I made a mental note: if I ever needed some cash, I knew where to find a trick.

***

Memphis

"I'on wanna hear no gagging or choking," I said to Skittles as she knelt in front of me. I cut a hole in my boxers to make it easier for my dick to slip out.

Skittles stroked me to get me hard. After Lil D and Ninety-Nine talked som' sense into Lil Ru, he finally respected the game and got out the way. I had my old-school potna Reese, and the homie Mack holding Jigga while we did our thing. I had to pay a white boy to let me use his cell only 'cause his cell was a blind spot. At first, Skittles was playing all scared and shit. I wasn't tryna hear non' of that 'I'm scared' shit. After a little persuasion, she yielded, with my dick stuffed in her mouth.

She stared into my eyes as she worked her tongue around the plump head. I turned my head to her shoes to prevent myself from looking at her ugly face. She kissed the head of my dick.

"You like that dick, don't you?" I asked.

She nodded and said, "Muhuh!" She went back to work like her break was over. I thought about how she was sucking my dick; it reminded me of Money Bagg Yo:

'She ate the dick through my underwear (uh)—'

Right when I got ready to push her tongue to the back of her throat, my security team yelled that the cross count was coming on the wing. Skittles jumped up and tried to kiss me. I stiff-armed her like I was Derrick Henry, and ran back to my cell.

I eased in my cell and slid the door, making it look like it was closed. I sat on the edge of my bed, facing the bars. I stuck my legs out the bars and pretended to be reading. I heard A-D before I saw her as she stopped and greeted my neighbor. I looked up as she walked in front of my cell.

"I thought you'd be out of the cell," she said.

"Why'd you think that? It ain't like you working over here."

She smiled.

"Hey, Kingpen," she greeted my celly. He nodded at her.

"Oh, before I forget, I have something to tell you," she said.

"What's up?"

"I was doing my count on G-Wing a minute ago, and this dude was in cell counting a lot of money. He tried to give me some but I didn't take it." She smiled hard.

"Did you like what you saw?"

"I mean it was money. It didn't impress me. Like I told him, five grand wasn't shit to a bitch like me." I looked at her. She thought she was smarter than the average dummy. She didn't know that I was the one that invented the game. She couldn't play a nigga that had all the cheat codes.

"You talkin' 'bout Sinbad, the nigga that stay on two row?" She looked at me surprised. "How you know?"

The other day I had ran out of tobacco, not wanting to go without, I told Sinbad I would send him $50 for $50 worth of tobacco. He shot me down. I then told him I would send him $100 for $50 worth. Thinking that head a duck, he said yes. I shot the money in less than a minute to show him it wasn't a money shortage on my end.

I knew it had to be the same guy. Sinbad had been gone for some time now, which meant he had the old-school penitentiary game. The ol' bait game. Show a young broke bitch some money and watch her squirm. That was the big difference between the old-school tricks, and a young finesser like me. Don't get me wrong. I applauded the cat for making ends meet with the pen, but as a finesser, I could never tilt my hat to him. His game was flash and dirty mack. Mine was persuade and blow. My game wasn't simple; it was beyond complicated. Niggas wondered how I bagged the baddest bitch on the unit, for those that knew. Then they wonder how I had a snow bunny on the side. Like I say, it's complicated. I was from the land of pimping. It ran through my bloodline. I had an uncle who had eighteen kids by ten different baby mamas. Neither put him on child support, and each baby mama got along. Pimping at its finest!

But to my point. I was a real pimp, a persuader. I broke hoes down and rebuilt them to my liking. I never flashed money. My job isn't to pay them, not then; their job was to pay me. Even when it was time to start dropping off, I wouldn't pay. Weeks and weeks of me gaming my bitch up, and I wouldn't have to pay. Why? Believe me when I say there's a thing about loyalty. If she's loyal, she'll feel obligated to give me every one of my needs. Before I'll ever have to, she'll ask, "Do you need anything?"

To answer her question from earlier, I replied: "I wasn't a hundred percent it was him, but you just confirmed it."

"You mad about it?" she asked.

"Why would I be mad?"

"You seem mad," she said.

The reason I was mad was because she had ruined my nut. I didn't give two fucks about flashin' money. I was too busy tryna push a bitch tonsils back.

"If you think I'm mad, so be it. But, kick rocks before niggas start watching us." She huffed and stormed away.

As soon as I knew she was off the wing, I left my cell and walked down the stairs and leaned on the dayroom bars. Skittles was sitting in the dayroom at a table, her legs were wide open, her pussy looked fat. She looked at me and smiled.

"Are you ready for round two?" I asked. She nodded. "Next count, okay?" She nodded and smiled. I sat on the cooler and slid it close to the dayroom bars.

"Why haven't you called me?" she asked.

"I'on got the number."

"I gave it to you, remember." I actually thought she was bullshitting that day she had given me her number.

"Write it down, I'ma call you tonight." She tore a piece of paper off an old count sheet and scribbled her number down. She placed it on the dayroom bars. I grabbed it, then tucked it in my sock.

"By the way, my name is Joshua," I said. She shook her head in embarrassment. I knew she felt like a slut for not knowing my name.

She told me her name as we rode for the next hour or so. She told me about her family, her daughter, and how she and Ms. Raven were best friends. When she asked about me to confirm if I was the very nigga Ms. Raven had been talking about, I simply said:

"I'm that nigga!"

Chapter Twenty-Nine

A Week Later

Lt. McFee

I was medically discharged from the hospital. I was only left with a slight limp. When Baby G and C.O. Patricia kicked my ass, they shattered my knee. I endured the pain of surgery, and twenty stitches to fix my knee. I had to walk with crutches, and bathe with my leg in a trash bag, but I was alive.

As for Patricia, no one has heard from her. As I was laying on the floor unconscious, she snuck out the building and left the state. Baby G has been charged with assault on an officer. I had him shipped to the Roach Unit. Last I heard, he was about to go to court to receive some more time because surely, I pressed charges. I didn't tell anyone about them having sex. I figured that would only heighten the amusement and give Baby G more stripes. He was already known for kicking my ass. I didn't want to make him look like Superman.

My co-workers thought I wasn't coming back to work. Everyone thought I'd got beat so badly that I would be scared straight and retire. Not Sean McFee. I was going to retire alright, as the warden. I had a job to do. A list of dirty C.O.'s and inmates to catch. And next up was Memphis.

"I've been hearing his name here and there. Inmates that claim to be gangsta, killers, and hustlers would drop I-60's on him saying that he was selling K2 and cell phones. I received one I-60 saying that he had two different C.O.'s that worked the same card, and the same shift. Now, that was a first for me. Not on my watch!

For the past few days, I've been watching him on camera. Watching his every move, who he communicated with. Who comes to his cell. How many times he uses the dayroom phone. He seemed to sleep the entire first shift away, which was smart, because I worked the first shift. When he came out at night to clean, he had the same routine: Sweep the trash, mop. Then workout. Watch

ESPN, then I wouldn't see him on camera for hours at a time. Where would he go? I'm still trying to piece it together.

***

Hotboy

I felt good that everything was working out well. Eastwood's been moving everything I sent his way. I had to get a new cash app to keep the bank off my ass. After me and Gabby did our thing a week back, I haven't heard from her, and she hasn't stopped by the house like she used to. I guess that was the last time we would ever see each other. But Stephanie—let me tell you about her. The next morning after I got home, she sucked my dick like an elephant sucks water. She rode my dick for hours and she cried the whole time. When I asked her why she was crying, she replied, "Cos you're mine."

The next day, she started packing all of our important stuff. I told her I was in the final stages. One last drop, and we would be set. I convinced her to go ahead and leave without me. I would have to take the back roads. She could fly straight through.

Now I was sitting at home with Lakewood as we took two cold *Coronas* to the head while watching the Super Bowl.

"So, you really fin' to leave?" Lakewood asked as he sat his half empty beer down.

"I'on have a choice. If anyone ever recognize me, I'm either dead or I'm going back to prison."

"So, this is it, our last ride?"

"You can always come with us."

He shook his head. "When we were in the pen', being around all them Mexicans had me paranoid. I damn sho'll ain't 'bout to move to their homeland."

I laughed. "I guess this is it then."

Lakewood picked up his beer and held it out. "To freedom," he said.

"To freedom!"

176

***

Eastwood

I wasn't one to count my chickens before they hatched, but I could already taste the freedom on my taste buds. I was a week away from never seeing the inside of a cell ever again. And boy, was I ready! I had already started giving shit away. I couldn't even stomach anymore commissary. Let alone look at another soup.

I had been informed of the last drop that was on the way. This would be the biggest one yet. Sixty phones, thirty chargers, forty cans of tobacco, two thousand sheets of K2 and sixteen ounces of the liquid K2 spray to make more. Stretch was excited. Since he started making a little money, he's been about to send some money home to his baby mama and daughter. Plus, he's been able to trick off with this lil' white C.O. he won. He let me see some snapchat videos of the thick ass white hoe. She was a straight nympho. Piercings on her titties, and she had one of the prettiest pussies I've ever seen. Every time I saw her face to face, I wanted to fuck her, but Stretch was my guy, so I let her make it.

People kept asking me why I didn't come to the dayroom anymore. I kept telling them I was exhausted from the working in the sign shop. But really, I wasn't tryna be in the dayroom just in case something popped off. I wouldn't be able to escape from seg'.

Kingpen

Chapter Thirty

Memphis

"Hello," I spoke into the dayroom phone. Jessica answered in tears. "What's wrong, ma?"

"She's gone!" she sobbed.

"What, what do you say?" I pressed the volume button on the phone.

"She's dead! My baby girl is dead!" I sank to my knees and cried.

"No-oo!" I cried, not wanting to believe it.

"She asked about you, right before she took her last breath." Her words cut me like a knife. "Josh!"

I didn't answer her. It was like my world had ended. Shattered into a million pieces. Like my heart had stopped beating. Like my purpose on earth was gone, never to return.

"Say something, please!" she cried. "I need you right now!" she begged. I didn't know what to say; I was at a loss for words.

"I'ma call you back." I hung the phone up before she could protest. I hung up because I couldn't do or say anything to make her feel better. I couldn't hold and comfort her, telling her everything would be okay. So, I hung up.

I stomped out the dayroom, tears streaming down my face. Ms. Raven looked at me. I walked past her to Big Tank's cell. He was one of the few people that knew Princess was sick. "What's up, boy?" he asked. My tears started falling like a waterfall. I started to cry like a baby. He looked at me for the first time. "What, aww man, damn!" He knew the answer to my tears before I could tell him.

"She's gone, family. My Princess is gone!" I felt like I was about to pass out.

"Stay strong, nephew. You gotta stay strong." Big Tank tried to console me.

Being strong was the last thing on my mind. I wanted my babygirl. To hold her, kiss her, tell her I love her and I'll always be with her. To read to her over the phone before she went to bed. To hear her voice one last time. To kiss both cheeks, just so she could say I missed her lips. To see her smile.

I cried until my head started hurting. I was sent to the unit chapel. The chaplain called the hospital where Jessica was at. The hospital where Princess was lying lifeless in. After confirming her death, the chaplain typed it in the computer, then sent emails to the majors and warden along with the psych department.

Then he said, "I want you to pray, son. God don't make no mistakes."

I stood up and walked out of his office. God had made a big mistake. He took the only love I've ever known. As I stood in the chapel, other inmates stared at me wondering why I was crying. Everyone knew me as the happy, always joking inmate. Now I was standing in front of them with teary eyes. It was amazing how fast the news had traveled. People were walking in the chapel, giving me their prayers and condolences. As I walked back to the wing, people stared at me. I walked on the wing and went straight to my cell, tossing the covers over my head. I didn't want to talk or eat. I just wanted my Princess. But she was dead. And I wanted to be with her. Even if I had to die too.

***

A Day Later

Anastasia

"Big Tank, hey, unc!" I smiled as he walked in the chapel. I had requested to work the keys on E, F, G, H block, but they made me work the chapel instead. I was pissed at first because me and Memphis wouldn't get to enjoy our ritual night together.

I was just coming back to work from my three days off.

"Have you went to see Memphis?" Big Tank asked.

"Not yet, I just got to work. I was supposed to be here earlier, but my car wouldn't start.

"Have you heard?" he asked.

"Heard what?"

"His daughter passed away." He shocked me. I clasped my hands over my mouth.

"For real?" I asked.

He nodded. "Yesterday. Broke my heart to see that boy like that. I hate that for him. He ain't no saint, but he didn't deserve that."

I cried. I cried like his daughter was my own. I felt like shit. Last week, when Sinbad showed me that money, I told Memphis about it. After he got on my ass and told me to kick rocks, I went back to G-Wing and me and Sinbad started talking. We flirted, and I kinda led him on. Before the night was over, I gave him my number. I only did it because Memphis pissed me off. But now I feel like a slut, like I betrayed him.

"I have to see him!" I said as I stood up.

'No, give him a few days. Let him mourn." I cried harder.

"But I want to see him. I want him to know I'm here for him!" I cried.

"Calm down before someone sees you."

"I-I don't care, Tank! I love him." Big Tank put his hand on my shoulder, making me sit down.

"He knows, trust me. But he needs his time alone. He told me that, please." I nodded. "Wipe your face. I'ma tell him you're praying for him and I'll tell you when he finally comes around. Until then, behave!" I looked at him, wondering if he knew my dirty little secret, and if he did, would he expose it?

Chapter Thirty-One

Monday Morning

Memphis

The funeral came faster than I wanted it to. Today was the day every parent dreads. Today would be the last time I would see my Princess. I felt sick, like I had the bubble guts. My stomach was touching back. I haven't eaten for three days. All I did was sleep.

I woke up and prepared myself for the worst day of my life. I don't understand life. I thought the kids were supposed to bury the parents, not the other way around, but here I was dressed in crisp whites, getting ready to lay my daughter to rest. To make matters worse, I wouldn't be able to attend the funeral in person. The unit was under COVID lockdown, so no one was allowed to attend any family funerals. I gave the warden hell behind it, but the best they could do was a Skype video.

As I was let out the cell, it felt like I was walking the green mile. Like I was walking to my own funeral. Really, I was. Because to bury my daughter would be to bury the best part of myself.

I walked to the chapel and let my homeboy Jai pray for me to give me strength. I didn't know how I was going to make it. After we prayed, I walked to the Major's office where the video was set up. I wasn't going to be able to attend the burial, just the service.

"You ready?" the Major asked without looking at me. I really wasn't, but I nodded still. I didn't really have a choice. Jessica had already said that she needed me there, even if it was only through a video screen, and if I chicken out, she will kill me. What she didn't know was that I was already dead. I died right alongside my Princess. I was just a shell of a man walking around.

The Major sighed as she turned the camera on. I could see Jessica clear as day. She gave her phone to her father; I greeted him. We never really got along. But under the circumstances, we were experiencing the same hurt, so we respected each other for the moment.

"Be strong," he said as the funeral started. I sat back and cried as the choir sang beautiful, soulful songs about going home to be with the Lord. I looked to the side of me; the Major and her secretary were both crying.

Jessica's dad stood up with the phone in his hand. He stood beside Jessica as he escorted her to the front of the church. I wasn't ready to view the body, but I knew I never would be. Jessica's cries were loud, and heartbreaking. I held my eyes close as she cried; I was too afraid to open them. I opened them slowly to see my Princess. My heart melted. The little bit that I had left that was keeping me alive. My Princess laid in her casket; she looked like an angel. She wore a pink Louis Vuitton tutu with pink ballerina slippers. Her pink and white shirt had the words: *Daddy's Angel*, in bold letters.

Reading the words on the shirt made me break down. I ran out the room in tears and dropped down in the hallway, leaning my back against the wall. "You have to finish it, do it for your little girl," the Major said as she squatted beside me with teary eyes.

She helped me up as I would never be the same. My whole body felt numb. I felt dead. And that was all that was left for me to do, die.

***

Three days later, I was still numb to life. Jessica had gone crazy and was admitted to Green Oaks Mental Institute. Her father told me she tried to overdose on Ambien while in the bathtub. Thank God they caught her in time.

I had stayed cooped up in the cell as I cried for days until I couldn't anymore. Skittles had tried to get me out of my funk. But it didn't help. Anastasia had sent a couple of messages through Tank, but it didn't help. I ended up having Skittles bring me two packs of Newports, and two coke bottles full of Crown Royal, and I tried drinking the pain away.

I sat on the cooler drunk as I waited to see who would be working 2nd shift today. To my amazement, Anastasia walked on the wing. It was the first time I'd seen her since before Princess died. As she looked at me, she gave me a half smile.

"Hey, how you doing?" she asked.

"I'm good, I guess."

"I tried to come down here to see you, but Big Tank told me not to."

"I know. He told me."

"I asked to work over here tonight. I had to see you."

I smiled weakly. "Thank you. I need to see you." I told her how the funeral went. How I almost didn't make it through the whole thing. Once I finished, she was in tears.

"I love you," she said.

I looked at her and said, "I love you too." I knew it wasn't the truth, but I needed someone to love at the moment because I had lost so much love. I wanted her to replace the love I had lost. She would be the temporary piece to fill the spot that I would smash into place, forcing it to work.

For the next two hours or so, she got me out my funk. We damn near talked about everything. I was still feeling the effects from the Crown Royal. She stood in front of me as she sorted through the mail. The day room was packed, but everyone was minding their own business.

Staring at her, the way she looked so sweet, the way her lips glossed, made my dick hard. "Look," I said to her quietly as I pulled my dick out. I started stroking myself up and down. She looked at me in shock and said:

"Boy!" She laughed. "Stop!"

"Touch it."

"No, do you see all these people in the dayroom? You better stop before they see you."

"I bet you want to put this big ma'fucka in yo' mouth." She smiled.

"Don't test me," she said.

"I dare you!" She shocked me as she looked over her shoulder to the dayroom. She looked back at me and gripped my dick. She opened her mouth wide and placed her mouth over my dick. She closed her mouth and moved her head up and down. Her jaws made a popping sound as she took my dick out her mouth. I was shocked and now horny as hell.

"Don't ever dare me!"

Chapter Thirty-Two

The Following Morning

Lt. McFee

They say to take down an army, you have to first cut off the head. In my line of work, you catch a foot soldier, torture them until they break, and you'll know everything about the head.

"McFee on the wing!" an inmate yelled as I walked on H-Wing. My leg was still messed up badly, so I couldn't run to my destination like I wanted to, so if Stretch was doing something he had no business doing, he had enough time to put it up. I didn't come to lock him up though, just make him sweat.

As I made it to three rows, I stopped in front of his cell. He was sitting on the stool, his feet resting on the toilet seat. He was engaged in a deep conversation. But not with his celly, but on a cell phone.

I see why you're locked up, I thought to myself.

I stood there for another twenty seconds before he noticed me. Once he did, he knew he was busted. He didn't even try to flush; he knew it would be pointless.

"Wangolo, I need your assistance on H-Wing," I spoke into my walkie talkie.

I walked up to Stretch's cell; to my surprise, the door was already open. "Put your hands behind your back." He did. I cuffed him. On his desk was a phone, and what I knew to be K2. I stuck the phone in my side pocket and put the K2 in my other pocket. Wangolo walked up the stairs. "Don't let no one in, or out this wing. And watch this cell. I think there's more in here." He nodded.

As I walked Stretch down the stairs, another inmate asked, stretching, "What's up, bitch, you good?" Stretch smiled like he hadn't been caught with anything.

"Yea' ain't shit." He tried to sound cool.

As we made it to my office, I took his handcuffs off. "Have a seat," I said. I laid the phone and K2 on my desk. He shook his head, knowing he was going up shit creek without a paddle. Before I could interrogate him, he said:

"Look, lieu', I made parole. I got on FI-3. I'm due to be home with my daughter in the next sixty days. I'll give you whatever you want. Just—Just let me go home, please!"

I looked at the white boy who had red socks on. Tattoos covered his whole body. His image resembled a stone cold gangsta, but deep down, he was a rat. Master Splinter, Ratatouille, Stuart Little, Jerry. All the above.

Seeing that he was already ready to give up the goods, I toyed with him. "I don't think it works like that, see, I have the evidence I need to get you at least five more years, and if I send this to the lab, and it comes back positive for K2, you could get another five added on top of that." His face became as red as his socks.

"What do you want? The dirty C.O.'s? You want gang members? I'll give you Memphis, he's fucking with the black girl Davenport. He gets Newport, phone, everything. Who else, Skittles! She's fucking everybody! I'll give you the whole team. Hell, there is a massive drop coming through as we speak."

"Massive drop. Where! When!" He had my attention.

"Can you promise to let me go home?" he asked.

"You have my word. If you tell me about this massive drop, I'll guarantee you go home to your daughter."

Without further ado, Stretch gave up the whole operation. I could've lied to him and put him back in population. Everyone would know he snitched, but nothing would happen to him. Prison had changed. Instead of taking out the snitches, the gang members would rather take out their own. Pirus against bounty hunters, yet they were allies. I never understood it, but I like it. Because as long as they continued to run the real gangstas off, it made room for my implanted snitches that I had on every wing. My snitches would live stress-free while feeding me information on everything.

"Wangolo, meet me at the south shower with a metal detector!" I spoke into my walkie talkie.

I locked Stretch up in seg' and walked to the south shower. Wangolo met me as we waited at the south turn-out for the list of guys Stretch gave me that would bring in the massive drop.

The backdoor opened, six inmates, all Caucasians were smiling like they'd just won the lottery. Once they looked up and saw me, their smiles faded. Wangolo had the metal detector set up already.

"I want all of you to strip out," I said. They knew they were busted. Instead of trying to hide everything, they just started pulling it out, tossing it to the floor. The wrapped packages were so heavy, they made a loud thump.

Wangolo looked at me in awe. "How'd you know they'd have this?"

I smiled and said. "My secret weapon. A snitch!"

***

Eastwood

I listened as Lil D informed me that Stretch had been popped by McFee. I jumped up and started flushing every piece of contraband I had. I sent word to my hold man to stay on his P's and Q's. I didn't trust Stretch. Yea, I did business with him, but only because he had the avenue. Any white boy that leaves his organization—no, let me rephrase that. Any white boy that leaves his racist organization to be with a bunch of blacks that he once despised, couldn't be trusted. I knew it was only a matter of time before the hit squad ran down on us all.

"Fuck!" I yelled. I was only two days from escaping off the unit. "Why are they racking y'all up?" I asked.

"They say McFee popped some niggas coming through the back door with a lot of shit. Phones, tobacco, tune."

I shook my head in disgust. I knew the only way he'd found out about the drop, was out of Stretch bitch ass mouth. That fat bitch McFee wasn't shit without his squad of snitches. The sooner niggas figured that out, the sooner the game would be good.

I was praying that we didn't go on a thirty-day lockdown for the shit they found. Because in two days, I would have a free ride. A ride to freedom.

Concrete Killa 3

Chapter Thirty-Three

Memphis

Bang! Bang! Bang!

"Hey get up!" Grizints banged on my cell bars. "McFee wants to see you."

I yawned and stood up. I got dressed and brushed my teeth. As the door rolled, I knew this was about to be some straight bullshit.

"Kingpen, if they lock me up, pack all of my shit up for me. It's three letters in my bible already addressed. Put Jessica's in the mailbox for me. One is yours, but don't read it until Friday," I said. He nodded.

"I gotcha."

Grizints walked me down to Lt. McFee's office. As I walked inside, he told me to sit down. "You know why you're here, don't you?

"This parole, ain't it?" I played dumb like I didn't know who he was.

He smiled. "Good one, but no. Tell me about your penitentiary girlfriend."

"I'on know nothin' bout no girlfriends."

"Davenport, she's not your girlfriend?"

"I'on even fuck with black hoes!" I spat. I was lying, 'cause I had fucked the shit out of Anastasia's wet pussy. She wouldn't stop sending me videos of her twerking and playing with her pussy, so the first chance I got, I punished her pussy.

"I have video footage of you two. Proof that you and her have a relationship going on."

"So, what are you waiting on? If you got so much proof, write it up, 'cause I ain't got no'n to say!"

McFee smiled. "You know I've been hearing your name, Memphis, for a while. I'm finally able to say I got you."

"You ain't got shit! A case that is worse is G4. Mane, that ain't shit. Tell yo' snitch to do his homework better. I always cross my t's and dot my i's. Yo' snitches are dumb as fuck. They'll give a nigga they mama address, wife address, thinking we cool, not knowing this really the den of thieves. Trust nobody! Yet, they give it out, being friendly, forgettin' a nigga will one day be free!"

I hit him with the lyrics of Yo Gotti's *Trapped*:

"I heard my niggas talkin' 'bout me, whispers gettin' closer / Niggas say I ain't breaking bread, I don't even know you / All that shit I bought you niggas, all the shit I taught you, nigga / Lil' disloyal, ungrateful nigga, I'm thinkin' I should off you niggas / Learn the hard way, keepin' it real may cost a nigga / All that love and bruh-bruh shit, they gon' cross a nigga."

McFee went into a rage.

"Get the fuck up, you're going to seg', and I'm writing you an established relationship case. You think this is going to be a project for you, a game, but I'll show you! This isn't the FEDS, this is Beto, and I own Beto! I'ma have you shipped so far, it'll take you two days to drive the distance, so you better pick up on your Spanish!" he said furiously.

I stood up as he cuffed me. I don't care about none of that shit he's talking about. I continued rapping Yo Gotti so that he would get the point.

"Mama in the hood, you know you forced to move the house (Trapped) / You took niggas' work, they went and shot up mama house (Trapped) / You a selfish nigga, damn near took your mama out (Damn)

***

Anastasia

I was called into Lt. McFee's office. I had already heard he locked Memphis up. Thanks to Memphis' warning, Memphis had already prepared me for this day, so I was ready. As I walked in his office, I saw McFee, the warden and Captain Burtes. They showed me a video of me and Memphis talking. We were also doing what they called horseplaying. But really all I did was grab his arm and pull him out of my seat.

Damn, Memphis was right, the camera doesn't see in the corner, I thought to myself.

"Okay, and?" I said once the video stopped.

"Davenport, we know about your relationship with inmate Curry. The other night, C.O. Oge said he saw you and Curry in the corner doing something," McFee said.

"Prove it!" I boldly said.

"Check her car. I know she's hiding something," Captain Burtes said. I told her to keep her dildo-wearing ass away from me. The warden gave her permission to pat search me. Just what the dykin' ass bitch wanted. After coming up empty handed, they searched my car and found a liquor bottle on the floor.

"Look what we have here. This is a direct violation," McFee smiled. "First, we have a video of you and another inmate touching each other. You also refused to do your security checks, and now, this—" he held the bottle up. "Three write ups, which will be an automatic resignation. You'll lose your job." he said. I hated his fat ass. He knew I needed my job. I was tryna save enough money to get my body done. Ass shot, and a breast implant, then move to Houston. Without this job, I could kiss Houston goodbye.

"What do you want?" I sighed.

"Tell me what you know about inmate Curry, everything. All the dirty C.O.'s. Leave nothing out." He grinned.

I huffed and thought about it. I could've easily told him about Memphis hustling. I had seen it with my own eyes. I could say how I'd heard Memphis was messing with Skittles on the side.

"If I do, what'll happen to me?" I asked.

"We'll ship him. Send him to another unit. Once he's gone you'll be able to come back, but, until he's shipped, you'll be on leave without pay." I nodded and tossed my ID on the table. McFee smiled.

"Okay, here it goes! All I know is y'all can kiss my black ass! My daddy ain't raise no snitch! Fuck this job!" I slapped my ass and walked out. Behind me, I heard McFee say:

"Let her leave. She wants to save her image, instead of her job. Spread the word that she snitched. See how Memphis likes it!"

Chapter Thirty-Four

Hotboy

I stood outside Lt. McFee's barn as I waited for him to come home. This was the moment I've been waiting on, the end.

McFee's truck pulled up to his driveway. The night sky barely made my dark skin visible. As he got out his truck, he started for the front steps. I made a noise with my feet against the gravel; he turned. "Who's there?" he asked, scared. I stayed still. He started walking in my direction. Once he saw me, his color drained from his face.

I was dressed in all black from head to toe. "Kingsley!" he said almost in a whisper. "Please forgive me," he begged. He actually thought he was seeing a ghost.

He walked closer. "I know you never liked me, and I understand. But, I was always only doing my job. I never meant to hurt anyone physically. You have to understand that. Don't haunt me forever. You're free now, rest in peace."

I raised my arm in the dark night. A .38 special with its handle wrapped in black tape was in my hand. "You rest in peace."

Pow! Pow! Pow! Pow! I emptied all six shots in his body. I stood over him to make sure he wasn't still breathing. Once I saw that he was extinct, I jumped in my car and prepared myself for the final act.

***

Eastwood

All night I stayed up, waiting anxiously for the sun to come up. I was sitting in the dark like a kid on Christmas morning. When the sun finally rose, I was one of the first ones out of the cell for work. I had a new walk, a little pep in my step.

The whole day at work, I kept looking at my watch. Hotboy was due to pull up with the trash truck at 10:00. I only had fifteen minutes left to make my move.

"Sir we need some more rags in our department. Could you take me to go get some?" I asked my boss as he was bringing his turkey sandwich to his mouth. My boss was lazy, so I knew him getting up to take me to get some rags would be out of the question. Especially being that he was eating.

"Go on, I'll call and let them know you're on the way," he said as he picked up the walkie talkie.

I smiled as I walked out the gate. Mr. Terry let me out the gate and watched me until he was out of sight. I had a sledge with me to carry the rags with, but unbeknownst to them, they'll never get any rags, and they'll never see me ever again.

The trash truck pulled into the unit. I smiled. Right on time! I stashed the sledge and hid behind the dumpster. As the trash truck pulled around, it parked with the back end to me. I heard a door open.

"Eastwood" Hotboy called my name. Seeing his face made me feel proud. There were still a few real niggas left. I crouched. We couldn't embrace just yet.

"Look, when I start filling the dumpster up, jump in the back and I'ma thro' trash on you. I know it smells bad, but they're all we got to work with. Once I finish, Ronnie will pull the lever down just enough to block you. That way, once we're on our way back out the gate, they'll never see you." I nodded.

Hotboy started throwing trash bags inside the back of the trash truck. "Now!" he said. I jumped my fat ass in the back and landed on top of a bunch of stinking trash. Even though it smelled awful, I still smiled.

After he finished with the last bag, he stood on the driver's side so he could see Ronnie's face. Hotboy raised his hand as the door started closing, smashing trash on top of me. Hotboy closed his hand into a fist, and the door stopped

"Next stop, freedom!" Hotboy said.

Chapter Thirty-Five

Memphis

I sat in the cell alone on T-Wing as I practically went crazy, thinking of my daughter. Knowing I'll never be able to see her again drove me mad. I felt like a psych patient. Then my so-called homies got down on me. Niggas I thought would keep it one hunnit stole my phone and dope. Rank wouldn't let me use the phone to check up on Jessica; shit was crazy.

Anastasia had started sending me Jpays about how she loved and missed me. Bitch didn't know I had already gotten wind of the fat pig McFee that she had snitched. I wrote her back to let her think everything was cool. I had to play a sucker to catch a sucker. I wasn't trippin'; it was all a part of the game. Everybody couldn't be real. In the game, you had only dope boys in the pen, like, where's the smokers—they don't exist anymore? Where's the disloyal ma'fucka's? Everyone all of sudden, loyalty over everything.

I didn't give a fuck though; I had something they didn't have. Two badass shanks. Made them myself. Back ma'fucka's too. Made it out of real glass. I made them in the image of lightning bolts, so once they're inside you, the only one that can remove them is the doctor. I made two of them, and named them, *Bad* and *Bitch*.

A day ago, the porter pulled up on my cell telling me that Stretch had been moved back here with me. He was a couple of cells down. The fool had been so quiet when he moved on the wing; I never noticed until he walked by my cell to go to the shower.

On T-Wing, there are showers on each row. But, we are only able to go one at a time in handcuffs. Once we get inside the shower, the C.O. will uncuff us. Earlier I paid the porter to stuff the two row shower door with tissue, so once it's closed I could pop it back open. Stretch was already in the shower on three rows.

As the guard took me to the shower on two rows, I turned my back so she could uncuff me. After he uncuffed me, he closed the shower door and yelled: "Three row shower, you ready?"

"Yea!" Stretch replied.

As I watched the guard walk up the stairs, I silently popped the door open. I pulled my *Bad* and *Bitch* out. I waited for the sound of the handcuffs. As I heard the cuffs lock around Stretch's wrist, I waited. My blood was pumping. Stretch came down the stairs in front of the C.O., his hands were behind his back. As soon as he came close to my shower, I slid the door open and raised the shanks. The C.O. saw the look in my eyes, the rigid shanks, and took off running.

"Memphis, please! I didn't snitch on you!" Stretch yelled.

I stabbed him in the neck with *Bad*, and stuck *Bitch* in his heart. He squirmed in his handcuffs as if he was choking on his own blood. He tried to walk away, as he was leaning onto the guard rail. I kicked him over two rows. As his body hit the concrete, he smashed *Bad* and *Bitch* fully into his body. His body stopped fighting a fight it couldn't win.

I ran back to my cell and prepared myself. I knew I was probably going to get my ass kicked by every C.O. on the unit. And once they finished, the warden would ship me to Polunsky Unit and hide me in seg' for ten years. While I'm waiting for trial, I wouldn't be allowed no visits, phone calls, or commissary. Then ten years later, do five more years G5, non-contact visits, and only twenty-five dollars' commissary. And after that, ten years G4 and that's if they don't give me lethal injection. I had a feeling they'll stick the needle in me. That's why I planned on doing it myself. I would never give them crackers the satisfaction of saying they took me out of the game. Hell, I made the game, and now it was time to put the cheat codes in.

I grabbed my bedsheet and hung it from the top locker. The entire T-Wing was banging on their bars with their locker doors open and shouted as hard as they could. I rushed and tied my door down with another sheet.

As I made a noose with the sheet, I stood on the edge of the bunk and tied it around my neck. The hit squad and all the ranking officers ran to my cell with a camera and riot gear. I smiled at the camera. The warden yanked on the cell door, but I had it tied down so tight it'll take them at least ten minutes to untie it.

I looked into the camera. No tears, no more pain. I was already dead. I wanted to see my daughter one last time. I knew killing myself meant I wouldn't go to heaven, but at least I would get to see Princess at Heaven's gate before God sent me in the opposite direction.

"Curry, do not, do it!" the warden yelled. She sprayed her mace. That shit wasn't going to stop me. My mind was already made up.

I laughed, looking directly at the camera, and recited a line from Tupac's song—*Ghost.*

"You motherfuckers can't stop me / Even if I die, I'm gon' be a fuckin' problem / Do you believe in ghosts, motherfucker? / Real live black...ghosts!"

I took a step off the bunk. The sheet gripped my neck like a vice grip. I smiled as I made my body shake on purpose to clear all the air from my lungs. The warden yanked and yanked on the door, but it is already too late. Elvis had left the building!

***

Eastwood

As me and Hotboy rode in the back of a Maria Cookie truck, hidden behind boxes and boxes of cookies, I cried.

"What's good, family?" Hotboy noticed me crying.

"Shit crazy, family. You came back for a nigga."

"No man gets left behind. How can I enjoy my freedom when my day one is locked inside a cage! That shit doesn't make any sense."

"You think McFee will put two and two together once they notice I'm gone?"

Hotboy laughed. "Nawl, McFee's gone. He's probably in a crackers heaven at a Honky Tonk chanting the word *nigger.*"

I looked at him. "Damn, he's dead. Who did it?"

Hotboy smiled and said: "The Concrete Killa!"

Kingpen

Chapter Thirty-Six

The Final Chapter

Anastasia

I just received a letter from Memphis that Kingpen gave to me. I cried when I found out that Memphis had hung himself. I knew I wasn't loyal to him fully, but I did have love for him. I opened his letter and started reading.

Anastasia,
If you are reading this, that means I'm no more. I want to let you know you're a disloyal bitch. Yea', I know what the fuck right. I know about everything. I just played it cool. Thanks for the sloppy toppy. I'll jack off to our memories in hell. I heard you were cheatin' on me, it's cool. I heard you messed with the fool Sinbad too. I'm happy for you both. Tell him, if he loved you and you were my bitch, if he kissed you, then he sucked my dick too. Just so you know, you ain't play me, I was playing you from the jump, you and that bitch Skittles. So now y'all have something common; y'all both got played by a true pimp from Memphis. In the words of Money Bagg Yo: **"I don't got a heart, but fuck it, I'm paid / Lil A beat a body he fresh out the cage / I'm still the same nigga from minimum wage / They tryna keep up, so they stalkin' my page / They do what I say, they tryna get saved / They line up for me like they coppin the J's / I told her get right, start actin' your age / Can't believe you tried it / Bitch, you played."**
To the grave,
Memphis.

I shook my head as I ripped the sheet into shreds. I was torn. For one, Memphis died thinking I snitched on him. Not knowing I kept it too real. And secondly, he wrote that he was messing with Skittles. I always feel that they had something going on.

Kingpen

I wiped my face and tossed the letter in the trash. I was back at Beto, once Memphis died. Everyone found out that McFee was killed outside his home. Once the new staff came, a lot of the rank got fired for the way they handled Memphis' death. I did what I had to do to get my job back. It was hard the first week; the place reminded me so much of Memphis. But now that he's gone I'm able to pursue my fling with Sinbad. Sometimes I could see Memphis' face. It's crazy, like, he's a ghost!

***

Kingpen

I sat in the cell alone as I typed on my typewriter. When Memphis told me he had something that I could put in a book, I didn't expect the story to be that live. I had no choice but to type it up and make a killing off of his story.

The three letters Memphis told me to get, one was for Anastasia. One was for his babymama Jessica, who was still in the mental institute. And the other one was for me.

Kingpen,
I hope you don't think I'm no less than a man for the way I went out. Shit was just fucked up, fo 'real, mane. I just couldn't take it no more. But I had to let you know, as much as I hated that tck tck tcking on yo' typewriter, you got a helluva gift. Don't ever stop, no matter what the next hating ass nigga say. They just mad that they didn't think of it first. They really just mad 'cause you got a comma after yo' zeroes and a comma after that. Real shit, fuck 'em. Tell Lil D I said to keep his rap shit up. Tell Chi-town to stay in the kitchen. Tell BooBoo to change his ways; he can't go home like that.

Tell Skittles when you see her, her pussy look like blue waffle. And mane, do me a real favor. Let them niggas know I ain't kill myself behind no pussy, or 'cause I got jammed up. A nigga was just exhausted. Let 'em know that even though I'm no more, I'll always live through yo' books. Make sure that you keep me alive. Kingpen,

you're a real nigga, and I pray you'll die a real nigga when the time comes.
    One Love,
    Memphis.

I folded Memphis' letter up and stashed it. I knew I was going to keep it forever. I wanted to grant him his last wishes. I knew he had a hard life, and the death of his daughter was the flame that burned his soul. But I was going to make sure to keep him alive. Now the whole world would read about him. They will be able to know how the whole story went from the beginning to the end!

The End

Lock Down Publications and Ca$h Presents assisted publishing packages.

BASIC PACKAGE $499
Editing
Cover Design
Formatting

UPGRADED PACKAGE $800
Typing
Editing
Cover Design
Formatting

ADVANCE PACKAGE $1,200
Typing
Editing
Cover Design
Formatting
Copyright registration
Proofreading
Upload book to Amazon

LDP SUPREME PACKAGE $1,500
Typing
Editing
Cover Design
Formatting
Copyright registration
Proofreading
Set up Amazon account
Upload book to Amazon

Advertise on LDP Amazon and Facebook page

Submission Guideline

Submit the first three chapters of your completed manuscript to ldpsubmissions@gmail.com, subject line: Your book's title. The manuscript must be in a .doc file and sent as an attachment. Document should be in Times New Roman, double spaced and in size 12 font. Also, provide your synopsis and full contact information. If sending multiple submissions, they must each be in a separate email.

Have a story but no way to send it electronically? You can still submit to LDP/Ca$h Presents. Send in the first three chapters, written or typed, of your completed manuscript to:

LDP: Submissions Dept
Po Box 944
Stockbridge, Ga 30281

DO NOT send original manuscript. Must be a duplicate.

Provide your synopsis and a cover letter containing your full contact information.

Thanks for considering LDP and Ca$h Presents.

<u>NEW RELEASES</u>

MOB TIES 6 by SAYNOMORE
A GANGSTA'S PAIN 2 by J-BLUNT
TREAL LOVE by LE'MONICA JACKSON
FOR THE LOVE OF BLOOD by JAMEL MITCHELL
CONCRETE KILLA 3 by KINGPEN

Kingpen

KINGPIN KILLAZ IV

STREET KINGS III

PAID IN BLOOD III

CARTEL KILLAZ IV

DOPE GODS III

Hood Rich

SINS OF A HUSTLA II

ASAD

RICH $AVAGE II

By Martell Troublesome Bolden

YAYO V

Bred In The Game 2

S. Allen

CREAM III

THE STREETS WILL TALK II

By Yolanda Moore

SON OF A DOPE FIEND III

HEAVEN GOT A GHETTO II

By Renta

LOYALTY AIN'T PROMISED III

By Keith Williams

I'M NOTHING WITHOUT HIS LOVE II

SINS OF A THUG II

TO THE THUG I LOVED BEFORE II

IN A HUSTLER I TRUST II

By Monet Dragun

QUIET MONEY IV

EXTENDED CLIP III

THUG LIFE IV

By **Trai'Quan**

Kingpen

THE STREETS MADE ME IV

By **Larry D. Wright**

IF YOU CROSS ME ONCE II

By **Anthony Fields**

THE STREETS WILL NEVER CLOSE IV

By K'ajji

HARD AND RUTHLESS III

KILLA KOUNTY III

By Khufu

MONEY GAME III

By Smoove Dolla

JACK BOYS VS DOPE BOYS II

A GANGSTA'S QUR'AN V

COKE GIRLZ II

By Romell Tukes

MURDA WAS THE CASE II

Elijah R. Freeman

THE STREETS NEVER LET GO II

By Robert Baptiste

AN UNFORESEEN LOVE III

By **Meesha**

KING OF THE TRENCHES III
by **GHOST & TRANAY ADAMS**

MONEY MAFIA II

LOYAL TO THE SOIL III

By **Jibril Williams**

QUEEN OF THE ZOO II

By **Black Migo**

THE BRICK MAN IV

By King Rio

VICIOUS LOYALTY III

By Kingpen

A GANGSTA'S PAIN III

By J-Blunt

CONFESSIONS OF A JACKBOY III

By Nicholas Lock

GRIMEY WAYS II

By Ray Vinci

KING KILLA II

By Vincent "Vitto" Holloway

BETRAYAL OF A THUG II

By Fre$h

THE MURDER QUEENS II

By Michael Gallon

THE BIRTH OF A GANGSTER II

By Delmont Player

TREAL LOVE II

By Le'Monica Jackson

FOR THE LOVE OF BLOOD II

By Jamel Mitchell

<u>Available Now</u>

RESTRAINING ORDER **I & II**

By **CA$H & Coffee**

LOVE KNOWS NO BOUNDARIES **I II & III**

By **Coffee**

RAISED AS A GOON I, II, III & IV

BRED BY THE SLUMS I, II, III

BLAST FOR ME I & II

ROTTEN TO THE CORE I II III

A BRONX TALE I, II, III

DUFFLE BAG CARTEL I II III IV V VI

HEARTLESS GOON I II III IV V

A SAVAGE DOPEBOY I II

DRUG LORDS I II III

CUTTHROAT MAFIA I II

KING OF THE TRENCHES

By **Ghost**

LAY IT DOWN **I & II**

LAST OF A DYING BREED I II

BLOOD STAINS OF A SHOTTA I & II III

By **Jamaica**

LOYAL TO THE GAME I II III

LIFE OF SIN I, II III

By **TJ & Jelissa**

BLOODY COMMAS I & II

SKI MASK CARTEL I II & III

KING OF NEW YORK I II,III IV V

RISE TO POWER I II III

COKE KINGS I II III IV V

BORN HEARTLESS I II III IV

KING OF THE TRAP I II

By **T.J. Edwards**

IF LOVING HIM IS WRONG...I & II

LOVE ME EVEN WHEN IT HURTS I II III

By **Jelissa**

WHEN THE STREETS CLAP BACK I & II III

THE HEART OF A SAVAGE I II III

MONEY MAFIA

LOYAL TO THE SOIL I II

By **Jibril Williams**

A DISTINGUISHED THUG STOLE MY HEART I II & III

LOVE SHOULDN'T HURT I II III IV

RENEGADE BOYS I II III IV

PAID IN KARMA I II III

SAVAGE STORMS I II III

AN UNFORESEEN LOVE I II

By **Meesha**

A GANGSTER'S CODE I &, II III

A GANGSTER'S SYN I II III

THE SAVAGE LIFE I II III

CHAINED TO THE STREETS I II III

BLOOD ON THE MONEY I II III

A GANGSTA'S PAIN I II

By **J-Blunt**

PUSH IT TO THE LIMIT

By **Bre' Hayes**

BLOOD OF A BOSS **I, II, III, IV, V**

SHADOWS OF THE GAME

TRAP BASTARD

By **Askari**

THE STREETS BLEED MURDER **I, II & III**

THE HEART OF A GANGSTA I II& III

By **Jerry Jackson**

CUM FOR ME I II III IV V VI VII VIII

An **LDP Erotica Collaboration**

BRIDE OF A HUSTLA **I II & II**

THE FETTI GIRLS **I, II& III**

CORRUPTED BY A GANGSTA I, II III, IV

BLINDED BY HIS LOVE

THE PRICE YOU PAY FOR LOVE I, II ,III

DOPE GIRL MAGIC I II III

By **Destiny Skai**

WHEN A GOOD GIRL GOES BAD

By **Adrienne**

THE COST OF LOYALTY I II III

By Kweli

A GANGSTER'S REVENGE **I II III & IV**

THE BOSS MAN'S DAUGHTERS I II III IV V

A SAVAGE LOVE **I & II**

BAE BELONGS TO ME I II

A HUSTLER'S DECEIT I, II, III

WHAT BAD BITCHES DO I, II, III

SOUL OF A MONSTER I II III

KILL ZONE

A DOPE BOY'S QUEEN I II III

By **Aryanna**

A KINGPIN'S AMBITON

A KINGPIN'S AMBITION **II**

I MURDER FOR THE DOUGH

By **Ambitious**

TRUE SAVAGE I II III IV V VI VII

DOPE BOY MAGIC I, II, III

MIDNIGHT CARTEL I II III

CITY OF KINGZ I II

NIGHTMARE ON SILENT AVE

THE PLUG OF LIL MEXICO II

By **Chris Green**

A DOPEBOY'S PRAYER

By **Eddie "Wolf" Lee**

THE KING CARTEL **I, II & III**

By **Frank Gresham**

THESE NIGGAS AIN'T LOYAL **I, II & III**

By **Nikki Tee**

GANGSTA SHYT **I II &III**

By **CATO**

THE ULTIMATE BETRAYAL

By **Phoenix**

BOSS'N UP **I , II & III**

By **Royal Nicole**

I LOVE YOU TO DEATH

By **Destiny J**

I RIDE FOR MY HITTA

I STILL RIDE FOR MY HITTA

By **Misty Holt**

LOVE & CHASIN' PAPER

By **Qay Crockett**

TO DIE IN VAIN

SINS OF A HUSTLA

By **ASAD**

BROOKLYN HUSTLAZ

By **Boogsy Morina**

BROOKLYN ON LOCK I & II

Kingpen

By **Sonovia**
GANGSTA CITY
By **Teddy Duke**
A DRUG KING AND HIS DIAMOND I & II III
A DOPEMAN'S RICHES
HER MAN, MINE'S TOO I, II
CASH MONEY HO'S
THE WIFEY I USED TO BE I II
By Nicole Goosby
TRAPHOUSE KING **I II & III**
KINGPIN KILLAZ I II III
STREET KINGS I II
PAID IN BLOOD **I II**
CARTEL KILLAZ I II III
DOPE GODS I II
By **Hood Rich**
LIPSTICK KILLAH **I, II, III**
CRIME OF PASSION I II & III
FRIEND OR FOE I II III
By **Mimi**
STEADY MOBBN' **I, II, III**
THE STREETS STAINED MY SOUL I II III
By **Marcellus Allen**
WHO SHOT YA **I, II, III**
SON OF A DOPE FIEND I II
HEAVEN GOT A GHETTO
Renta
GORILLAZ IN THE BAY **I II III IV**
TEARS OF A GANGSTA I II
3X KRAZY I II

STRAIGHT BEAST MODE

DE'KARI

TRIGGADALE I II III

MURDAROBER WAS THE CASE

Elijah R. Freeman

GOD BLESS THE TRAPPERS I, II, III

THESE SCANDALOUS STREETS I, II, III

FEAR MY GANGSTA I, II, III IV, V

THESE STREETS DON'T LOVE NOBODY I, II

BURY ME A G I, II, III, IV, V

A GANGSTA'S EMPIRE I, II, III, IV

THE DOPEMAN'S BODYGAURD I II

THE REALEST KILLAZ I II III

THE LAST OF THE OGS I II III

Tranay Adams

THE STREETS ARE CALLING

Duquie Wilson

MARRIED TO A BOSS I II III

By Destiny Skai & Chris Green

KINGZ OF THE GAME I II III IV V VI

Playa Ray

SLAUGHTER GANG I II III

RUTHLESS HEART I II III

By Willie Slaughter

FUK SHYT

By Blakk Diamond

DON'T F#CK WITH MY HEART I II

By Linnea

ADDICTED TO THE DRAMA I II III

IN THE ARM OF HIS BOSS II

Kingpen

By Jamila

YAYO I II III IV

A SHOOTER'S AMBITION I II

BRED IN THE GAME

By S. Allen

TRAP GOD I II III

RICH $AVAGE

MONEY IN THE GRAVE I II III

By Martell Troublesome Bolden

FOREVER GANGSTA

GLOCKS ON SATIN SHEETS I II

By Adrian Dulan

TOE TAGZ I II III IV

LEVELS TO THIS SHYT I II

By Ah'Million

KINGPIN DREAMS I II III

By Paper Boi Rari

CONFESSIONS OF A GANGSTA I II III IV

CONFESSIONS OF A JACKBOY I II

By Nicholas Lock

I'M NOTHING WITHOUT HIS LOVE

SINS OF A THUG

TO THE THUG I LOVED BEFORE

A GANGSTA SAVED XMAS

IN A HUSTLER I TRUST

By Monet Dragun

CAUGHT UP IN THE LIFE I II III

THE STREETS NEVER LET GO

By Robert Baptiste

NEW TO THE GAME I II III

MONEY, MURDER & MEMORIES I II III

By **Malik D. Rice**

LIFE OF A SAVAGE I II III

A GANGSTA'S QUR'AN I II III IV

MURDA SEASON I II III

GANGLAND CARTEL I II III

CHI'RAQ GANGSTAS I II III

KILLERS ON ELM STREET I II III

JACK BOYZ N DA BRONX I II III

A DOPEBOY'S DREAM I II III

JACK BOYS VS DOPE BOYS

COKE GIRLZ

By **Romell Tukes**

LOYALTY AIN'T PROMISED I II

By Keith Williams

QUIET MONEY I II III

THUG LIFE I II III

EXTENDED CLIP I II

By **Trai'Quan**

THE STREETS MADE ME I II III

By **Larry D. Wright**

THE ULTIMATE SACRIFICE I, II, III, IV, V, VI

KHADIFI

IF YOU CROSS ME ONCE

ANGEL I II

IN THE BLINK OF AN EYE

By **Anthony Fields**

THE LIFE OF A HOOD STAR

By Ca$h & Rashia Wilson

THE STREETS WILL NEVER CLOSE I II III

Kingpen

By K'ajji

CREAM I II

THE STREETS WILL TALK

By Yolanda Moore

NIGHTMARES OF A HUSTLA I II III

By King Dream

CONCRETE KILLA I II III

VICIOUS LOYALTY I II

By Kingpen

HARD AND RUTHLESS I II

MOB TOWN 251

THE BILLIONAIRE BENTLEYS I II III

By Von Diesel

GHOST MOB

Stilloan Robinson

MOB TIES I II III IV V VI

By SayNoMore

BODYMORE MURDERLAND I II III

THE BIRTH OF A GANGSTER

By Delmont Player

FOR THE LOVE OF A BOSS

By C. D. Blue

MOBBED UP I II III IV

THE BRICK MAN I II III

THE COCAINE PRINCESS I II III IV V

By King Rio

KILLA KOUNTY I II III

By Khufu

MONEY GAME I II

By Smoove Dolla

A GANGSTA'S KARMA I II

By FLAME

KING OF THE TRENCHES I II

by **GHOST & TRANAY ADAMS**

QUEEN OF THE ZOO

By **Black Migo**

GRIMEY WAYS

By Ray Vinci

XMAS WITH AN ATL SHOOTER

By Ca$h & Destiny Skai

KING KILLA

By Vincent "Vitto" Holloway

BETRAYAL OF A THUG

By Fre$h

THE MURDER QUEENS

By Michael Gallon

TREAL LOVE

By Le'Monica Jackson

FOR THE LOVE OF BLOOD

By Jamel Mitchell

BOOKS BY LDP'S CEO, CA$H

TRUST IN NO MAN

TRUST IN NO MAN 2

TRUST IN NO MAN 3

BONDED BY BLOOD

SHORTY GOT A THUG

THUGS CRY

THUGS CRY 2

THUGS CRY 3

TRUST NO BITCH

TRUST NO BITCH 2

TRUST NO BITCH 3

TIL MY CASKET DROPS

RESTRAINING ORDER

RESTRAINING ORDER 2

IN LOVE WITH A CONVICT

LIFE OF A HOOD STAR

XMAS WITH AN ATL SHOOTER

Concrete Killa 3